LADY OF THE HIGHWAY

Book Three of The Highway Trilogy

DEBORAH SWIFT

© Deborah Swift 2016

Deborah Swift has asserted her rights under the Copyright, Design and Patents Act, 1988, to be identified as the author of this work.
All rights reserved.

No part of this book may be reproduced in any form or by any electronic or mechanical means, including information storage and retrieval systems, without written permission from the author, except for the use of brief quotations in a book review.

Quire Books 2022
First published 2016 by Endeavour Press Ltd.

Near the Cell, there is a well
Near the well there is a tree
And under the tree the treasure be

*Traditional Hertfordshire rhyme
about The Wicked Lady*

LADY OF THE HIGHWAY
CHARACTERS

Lady Katherine Fanshawe (Kate)
Ralph Chaplin – Kate's lover, a ghost
Abigail Chaplin – Kate's deaf maidservant
Elizabeth – Abigail's older sister
Martha – Abigail's younger sister
Thomas Fanshawe – Kate's husband, a Royalist
Sir Simon Fanshawe – Kate's stepfather (Thomas's uncle)
Cutch – Ralph's friend, an ostler
Mrs Binch – a cook
Constable Mallinson – a Parliamentarian
Jacob Mallinson – the constable's son
Jack Downall – a Puritan
Grice – former overseer of Markyate Manor

And the Diggers:
Owen and Susan Whistler
Seth and Margery Barton
Ben Potter

1

SPECTRES IN THE DARK

Kate
Winter 1651

THE LANTERN ON THE FLAG FLOOR gave out only a glimmer of light. I fastened the harness by feel, remembering how I'd seen the servants do it, hoping I'd done it right. Curses. It was taking too long. All the time I kept shooting a glance over my shoulder. The dark recess behind me made me nervous; something might be waiting, cloaked in liquid shadow, just out of sight.

I shook off the sensation and climbed up onto the trap. With a flick of the whip, Pepper, sensing my urgency, broke into a fast trot. I hoped he could see more than I could, as the hedges jolted past in a blur. Dusk had melted to darkness and the narrow rutted lane was pooled with the shadows of trees. The moon was yet to rise. There was no noise except the clatter of iron hooves and the creak of wheels on stones.

Past the village green, past houses with battened windows, down a stony bridleway until I came to a cottage on its own. A one-roomed cottage with a byre attached. Through the crack of the shutter I glimpsed the tremor of movement and a glow within, from a fire. I leapt down and hammered on the door.

'Who's there?' A wary voice.

'Katherine Fanshawe. Open the door.'

Silence from the other side.

I pounded with my fists. 'Mrs Binch! It's about my maidservant,' I cried. 'Abigail Chaplin. She's ill. She needs help.'

'Cease your banging! D'you want to wake the dead? Who else is with you?'

'Nobody. I'm alone. Don't you remember Abi?'

The scrape of the bar being lifted, and then the door swung open.

Mrs Binch, her hair pulled back into a long plait under her nightcap, kept one hand pressed on the jamb to keep me out. 'What's this about Abigail?' She did not curtsey to me, and her eyes were suspicious.

'She's been coughing these last five nights. I don't think she can stand much more.'

'Why? What's the matter?'

'She coughs like she can't catch her breath, like it will break her bones. And she's a fever. I've no skill in medicine.'

'Five nights, you say?' Mrs Binch pulled her knitted shawl tight across her chest and frowned. 'So you're expecting me to come out in the middle of the night, are you?'

'No. That's not what I meant,' I said. 'It's just…' This was awkward. Mrs Binch used to be my cook, but she had left me without notice, and now I was forced into asking her a favour. 'I'm not good with sick people,' I said. 'I don't know what to do, and she's so poorly. I know she liked you, and I'm afraid for her.'

Mrs Binch's expression softened. She opened the door wider, and hustled me inside.

She tutted through her teeth. 'All those deaths. It's not natural. And now Abigail. They're saying you're bad luck in the village.

My son thinks the Fanshawes are cursed. He won't like it if I go anywhere near the manor.'

'He doesn't have to know,' I said firmly. 'There's only Abi and I living there. Won't you hurry?'

'Hold your horses. I'm not your servant now, and an "if you please" would help. You can't just barge in here and expect me to drop everything to do your bidding.'

'Mrs Binch,' I gripped her by the arm, 'this is no time to argue. If you don't come soon, she might die.'

That settled it. Mrs Binch fixed me with an assessing gaze. Satisfied at last, she swung open the oak cupboard on the wall and picked out jars and pots, scrutinizing their contents. 'Have you any mint?' she asked.

'No,' I said, stamping my feet, wishing she'd hurry, 'I don't think so.'

'What about menthol? Or mustard?'

'No.' Markyate Manor had nothing. The cupboards were bare. 'Have you everything you need?' I said, but Mrs Binch would not be pressed. She disappeared into the back room and emerged fastening a warm wool skirt and bodice, before counting the items methodically into her basket. Finally I managed to bustle her out and help her up onto the trap.

'Don't drive too fast, mind. My old bones won't stand it,' she said.

I gritted my teeth and set off as fast as I dare. Now she was up there, there wasn't much Mrs Binch could do about it, and I was anxious about Abi, all alone in the big house. I'd left her sleeping, but I didn't want her to wake up and find the house empty, and me gone.

Pepper trotted at a lick through the lane, at my urgent flapping of the reins. I didn't know how long I'd been away, but every minute mattered.

'Slow down!' came Mrs Binch's voice from behind me.

As if he'd heard her, Pepper shied, and let out a neigh. An answering neigh from the darkness ahead.

I pulled Pepper to a halt, and listened.

'What's wrong?' Mrs Binch asked.

'I don't know, someone else on the road.' But I could see no lights from any carriage lantern. I slackened the reins and listened.

'Who's there?' I called.

Silence.

'Probably just one of Soper's horses in the field,' Mrs Binch said. But I was uneasy. Pepper's ears were back. Before us, the lane was a lightless tunnel. I thought of Abi, her chamber fire dwindling to ash whilst I was gone, and clicked to get Pepper going again. But he was spooked now, and skittish. Still, I drove him forward.

The trees leaned over us; the woods dense stripes of darkness each side. Ahead, a paler light marked where the tunnel of trees ended, so I slapped the reins to Pepper's neck to make him trot through. A flash of movement to my left and another horse shot out of the trees. Mrs Binch screamed. At the same moment, Pepper stumbled and veered, causing the trap to shudder.

In one glance my eyes took in a broad-shouldered man with a wide-brimmed hat shadowing his face. He was astride a huge horse; seventeen hands, if it was an inch. I took in all this, though something else had hooked my attention – the dull glint of a pistol, a miniature cannon, pointing right now at my chest.

'Your purse,' the stranger said. His voice, muffled by a kerchief, was low and hoarse as if he did not want to speak at all.

'I have no purse,' I said, mustering courage.

'Then I'll take what you do have.'

'Do as he says,' Mrs Binch's voice was high pitched with panic. I half turned to see her pushing the basket towards him.

'I have no purse,' I repeated.

A gasp from Mrs Binch. Another movement on my right. My

head whipped round. The second man was thinner and shorter than the first, but he was on foot. His pistol was cocked ready and his skinny white finger was resting on the trigger.

'Get down,' he said, his voice a nasal whine through the rag tied over his face. He sounded younger than the other.

I dropped down, my feet landing in a rutted puddle and the wet splashed cold up my ankles.

The smaller man strode towards me, but I barely saw him, my eyes were fixed on his gun. Suddenly, he shoved it in his belt, and startled, I looked up to see a pair of dark calculating eyes glinting a hand's span above me. His hands clamped down on my shoulders.

'I've nothing,' I cried. I squirmed to wrest myself away.

At my voice, he let go, stepped away, uttered a curse. 'What shall I do? It's Katherine Fanshawe.'

My blood seemed to stop in my veins. How did he know my name? But it was too dark to see his face properly, even if it had not been covered with a kerchief.

'Well, well,' the bigger man said. 'Best keep that ugly face hidden, then. And search her,' he commanded. 'Maybe she'll have something worth stealing.'

I froze, my insides recoiling, as the man before me pulled his hat lower, before he shot out a wiry hand to pinion me by the throat. His other palm slid over my bodice and skirts. Though his touch made me want to flinch, I stood proud. He would find nothing.

A sudden push and my back slammed hard against the trap. 'She's nothing on her. She tells the truth.' The smaller man's voice was unsteady.

'What about the old woman?' the big man said, kicking his horse forward and aiming his pistol at Mrs Binch's head.

'Please take it,' Mrs Binch said, pushing the basket towards him. 'Take it all. Just leave us alone.'

'See what she's got,' the highwayman called from his horse.

His accomplice searched through the basket, ripping bags open, scattering the contents, hurling the jars out onto the road. I could tell by his shaking fingers, that the younger man was nervous.

The mounted man rode over. 'Just chaff! Leave it, man. It's a waste of bloody time.'

How foolish I'd been to set out unarmed. If I could only get myself back into the driving seat… The thought had no sooner crossed my mind than the big man spoke again.

'Strip her,' he said. 'The gown'll be worth something, at least.'

The short man hesitated. 'I don't think—'

'Do it,' the big man snapped. 'It'll teach her a lesson.'

The shorter man swivelled back to me. 'Turn round,' he said, with sudden determination, nosing the pistol to my chest. He pushed me so my wooden stomacher was crushed against the iron wheel of the cart. I couldn't see his face.

A tug, as if I was being pulled from behind, then I saw the glint of a knife from the corner of my eye. He was going to kill me. I winced, expecting the knife to come to my throat. Rough hands pulled at my bodice. It came away in his hands.

He'd cut all the laces. The cold air blew through my shift.

Horrified, I crossed my arms over my chest. As he stepped away, he shoved the knife into his belt next to his pistol, and then passed the bodice to the mounted man, who picked over the green embroidered bodice with practised fingers, feeling the weight of the gold thread and embroidery. The sight made me angry.

'You forgot something,' I called boldly. 'The sleeves.'

'Ha! She's right,' the bigger man said, from the gloom of the trees. 'Best take them too.'

I jutted my chin and pulled the sleeves down with as much dignity as I could muster, casting them onto the ground.

The highwayman did not pick them up. He took a step

towards me, pushed me back against the cart until my back was to him once more. 'Don't look at my face,' he growled.

A shiver went up my spine. Would he strip me naked?

'No,' whimpered Mrs Binch, reading my mind.

'Shut your mouth.' The man on the horse leaned down to the cart and cuffed Mrs Binch a sudden blow with the barrel of his gun. Her hand flew to her face, her eyes flaring open with shock and fear.

'Leave her alone!' I cried, but my protests died, as the mouth of a gun jabbed against my back, cold through the muslin against my spine.

'And your skirt,' the short man said. 'Take it off.'

I untied the laces with shaking fingers, fumbling in my haste. I let it fall in a pool around my ankles. 'Step out,' he said.

I did as he asked, hearing Mrs Binch moaning in pain from the back of the cart. He scooped up the bundle of cloth and threw it over the withers of the bigger man's horse.

'Come here,' he said, pulling me backwards towards him. His voice was even hoarser now in my ear.

'Leave her,' the big man said. 'Don't be stupid, no matter how much you want her, you can't have her. D'you want everyone to know your name?'

The highwayman's hands clutched at my bare back through the muslin as he pressed himself towards me. His leather belt dug into my hips. His hands roamed my back. I felt his fingers find the scars. Suddenly he lifted up my hair, pulled the back of my shift down. I cringed away, ashamed, but his fingers found the welts on my back.

He turned me to face him, thrust me roughly back against the trap. He seemed to be searching my face, though I couldn't be sure. He pulled his kerchief further up over his nose. His eyes were sunk deep in shadow under his hat. With an angry gesture one hand tore at the neck of my shift. I heard the fabric rip. I panted for breath as he pressed himself towards me.

A wind, cold as ice, and sudden, as if a sea storm had arisen in an instant. A frisson like quicksilver shot up my spine. A creak, then a cracking noise. I looked up. The highwayman paused, the knuckles of his hand gripping tight to the fabric of my shift, tilting his head to listen.

Something was falling. There was no time to call out but he heard it at the same time as I did and stepped backwards just as a huge branch came crashing down. The gust as it hit the ground blew my shift flat against my legs.

We both stared at the branch, thick as a thigh, where it lay between us. The air vibrated with a strange feeling, as if someone was watching. The highwayman's eyes darted here and there, piercing the dark. The air felt thick as soup. I turned to look behind me, thought of Ralph.

A grumble of wheels in the distance, hooves.

It seemed to wake the highwayman from his trance. Hurriedly, he looked up, seeing no more danger he stepped over the branch, held the gun to my temple. 'I'll have you...' he whispered.

'A carriage,' the other man shouted, his horse sidestepping at the noise. 'Four-hander. The men we're after. And there'll be rich pickings. Leave her.'

I looked frantically back along the road. Twin carriage lights bobbed in the distance.

'Leave her I say!'

Unsure what was happening, I kicked and tried to shout, 'Help!' but the highwayman's hand, greasy with horse sweat and leather, clamped my mouth shut. Next moment I felt my feet lifted with surprising strength, as he took me under the arms and hurled me back onto the cart. My ribs hit the side, and I fell down into it, winded. Nausea threatened to overwhelm me.

A slap as he hit Pepper on the rump and a shout of 'Git!'

The cart lurched into motion and careered off down the lane. Driverless, Pepper broke into a canter and the cart rattled and jerked away. All knew was, I had to get into that driver's seat before the cart turned over or Pepper got a foot caught in the traces. I tried to stand but we were going too fast for me to balance, so I crawled forwards. It was disorientating, rattling through the dark, but I lunged forward, casting out the handle of the whip to try to hook the flapping reins.

Finally I had hold of them and pulled Pepper into a ragged walk. He was blowing, his neck frothed with white sweat. Just as I pulled up I heard a shot. My heart leapt in my chest.

The coach. They were holding up the coach.

More shots. I felt a glimmer of sympathy for whoever was behind us on the road.

'Don't stop! For Christ's sake, get us out of here,' groaned Mrs Binch.

Frightened they might come after us again, I drove Pepper on, away from the dark woods and towards the park and Markyate Manor. As I came around the bend in the drive, a blood-red harvest moon rose, huge as a sovereign, over the roof of the manor house. The house was oil-dark, like a hole in the horizon. My throat closed up as if I might cry. The men had taken our food and medicine. And inside the manor lay my only friend in the world, Abi, and what use were we to her now? A girl in a flapping shift, and an injured old woman?

2

GRIEF AND DREAMS

I HELPED Mrs Binch down from the trap and gave her my arm to steady her. In the house I found the kitchen fire still aglow, so once I'd guided her to a seat I lit tapers and candles.

Once we had some light I could see her face was purpled all down one side. A trickle of blood had dried to a crust on her cheekbone.

'Let me find some water to wash your face.'

'What did I tell you?' she said. 'My son was right. Bad luck rides pillion with you.'

I wrung out a cloth in the pail and held it out, but she shook her head. 'Now, I'm here, you'd best show me to Abigail.'

'Are you sure you're all right?'

'No. But maybe she's worse. Let's take a look, shall we?' She stood up, swayed slightly, but grasped the table for support. I went to take her round the waist, but she shrugged me off. Together we went up the stairs into my chamber where I'd left Abi coughing. Was it only a few hours since I'd left? It seemed like days. As we went up, I saw that Mrs Binch was thinner. We all were. The years of fighting and civil disorder had left us tired; food was scarce and women always the last to be fed.

Mrs Binch drew the candle closer to Abi's face, and even from here I could see Abi was ashen, her face grey as water against the sheets. I was used to giving orders, and expected them to be obeyed, but even I could not make someone live if they wanted to die. Even if she was my closest friend.

Her chest rattled as she breathed, like corn in a sieve. The sound filled me with dread. Mrs Binch turned Abi on her side but she barely reacted. She was like a limp leather bag, no fight left in her; her eyes were closed as if to shut out the world.

A bad sign. Abi was deaf and used her eyes to hear. The fact she could not find the will to open them meant she would be in a world of utter silence and darkness. Not that I could blame her. She had buried her mother and her baby brother together, and afterwards, her elder brother Ralph, who had died in a sword fight.

At the thought of Ralph, my heart contracted. The image of him rose up in front of me, his tousled blond hair and his ready smile. Grief at his passing made my stomach heave, and I had to go to the chamber pot to cough up bitter bile. A month or more I had endured this grief-sickness, along with a sense of loss so sharp it made me moan.

My house was full of ghosts. Markyate Manor had its wandering monk, its headless spectre, and now Ralph. I still could not believe him gone. I sat down heavily on the end of the bed. I must not cry.

I straightened the sheets angrily, pulling them taut, noticing how Abi's ribs showed through her thin shift. I knew she had lost weight, that she wouldn't eat, but for the first time I saw how thin she really was. The few blankets were rolled into a heap at the end of the bed, so I dragged them up over her shivering form.

Despite the chill, her forehead was burning to the touch. 'Don't you dare die,' I said through gritted teeth. Of course she couldn't hear me.

At the other side of the bed Mrs Binch turned away, her face grim.

'She'll be all right, won't she?' I asked.

Mrs Binch ignored the question. 'Fetch more wood. We must keep her warm. And I need to look in the larder.'

'It's empty,' I said.

'We'll see,' she brushed past me, one hand to her sore face, the other holding a candle. 'Boil water,' she called back. 'And fetch more blankets. And while you're at it, get dressed. Or you'll catch your death too, and I can't nurse the two of you.'

I was about to protest at being given orders, but shut my mouth. It was a relief to do something. I didn't want to think. My heart hammered from the thought of the two men in the woods. I still felt the touch of those rough fingers on my back. They'd known my name. I clutched my torn chemise together and shook the uneasy feeling away. I was well known round these parts. Many would know my name.

As I threw on warm skirts and a front-lacing bodice and sleeves, I remembered the falling branch. It was so odd. There'd been only a breath of wind before that, and then all of a sudden – that great gust. A prickling sensation, like needles inside my skull. I kept thinking of Ralph. My ordinary eyes couldn't see him, but I knew he was there. As certainly as a bird knows the dawn and begins to sing.

Even now, it was as if my chest was caving in at the thought of him. I pulled the laces tight and pressed my hand to the pain in my chest. I hadn't known love could be such agony. The loss of him was like waking to find yourself in another foreign country where you knew no one and where none of the language made sense.

I took a deep breath. I must put him from my mind and concentrate on Abi. It's what Ralph would have wanted, that I should look to his sister. She was like a sister to me too now. When I got back to the chamber with more blankets, the room smelt pungent. I suppressed the urge to gag. A bowl wafting steam stood next to the bed, and Mrs Binch was holding a vaporous cloth near Abi's nose.

'Camphor,' I said.

'Yes, from the master's clothes chest. She has more need of it than the moths, and there's little else. Does her sister still work at the apothecary's?'

'Elizabeth? Yes.'

'Then go there tomorrow, I'll write you a list.' Both of us ignored the fact I would have to ride down that highway again, though the unspoken fear was in both our eyes.

Why hadn't I sent a note to Elizabeth? I suppose because any fool could see that Abi and her sister didn't see eye to eye. 'I thought of that,' I said, 'but...'

'Money is it?'

I swallowed my pride. 'I can't pay her. Not unless we can sell something, and—'

'She'll surely give you credit, when she knows who it's for. Go at first light. But go careful. Go 'cross the fields, down the biddy bridleway. Don't risk the main highway.'

I did not reply. I'd go on the main highway if that was quickest.

Mrs Binch interrupted my thoughts, 'I'll sit with Abigail a few hours, mistress. You sleep. Doesn't do for us both to be awake.'

'If you're sure.' Strangely, I was glad to hear her use the familiar term 'mistress'.

She nodded and took her attention back to Abi. She sent me to rest, but I could not sleep. Slanted moonlight fell in bars across the floors, but I prowled the shadows, as if too much light might show up the hollow in my heart, as well as the dust.

I wandered into the main chamber noticing the mouldering candle stubs in the sconces. I ran my hand over the once smooth mahogany of the mantelpiece, now rough with gouges of musket fire. The house was battered and empty, and unloved.

I couldn't bear it. One day, I vowed, there would be a vase of roses just here, and a fire blazing, and chandeliers flickering beads of light across a polished table. One day, it would be a home again, filled with friends, and laughter and light.

Abi had to pull though. Dear God, hadn't I lost enough?

3

THE FANSHAWE LUCK

THE NEXT MORNING I saddled Blaze, my riding horse, and set off for Wheathamstead. Though it was slower, I went by the quiet bridleways. I did not want to come across the robbed coach or risk seeing those two men again. I wore a plain black worsted dress, and a plain velvet hat to hide the fact that there was nobody to dress my hair, and because my copper-coloured hair was like a beacon advertising who I was. With luck, I might pass for a village woman as I rode side-saddle across the common.

One or two men out in the fields close to the village stood up to stare, but daylight had washed the world of fear. Autumn sun burned through the mist, the cows grazed in heavy dew. A pigeon cooed from the distant woods. As I rode a wave of nausea made me sway in the saddle. I prayed to God I was not catching Abi's sickness.

I pulled Blaze up short and dismounted to vomit into a heap of autumn leaves at the side of the track. Afterwards I felt better, but wondered if it was grief, or whether my body was still trying to get rid of that feeling from the night before, the feeling of that filthy highwayman's hands on my bare skin.

When I got to the apothecary's I was surprised to see Elizabeth was not in mourning for Ralph. Instead she wore an amber linen dress, with a clean white waist-apron, and a frilled cap holding back her dark curly hair. Her chemise was cut low on the bosom, so that you could not help but notice the expanse of pale skin and cleavage in front. She looked up when I came in and her face closed in a scowl. She waited for me to speak.

I drew out the list I had written on Mrs Binch's instructions. 'All this, if you can,' I said. 'It's for your sister. She's in a bad way.'

'Why?' Elizabeth said, taking the list between finger and thumb, and eyeing it suspiciously. 'What ails her?'

'She can't stop coughing. And she's so weak. Ralph's death has knocked the straw out of her. Could be an infection of the lungs.'

'Has she seen anyone?'

I paused. I had promised Mrs Binch nobody would know she was there. 'No one,' I said.

'She was always sickly,' Elizabeth said. 'It's probably just a cold. She's a right malingerer. I'll give you a pinch of onion powder and ginger.'

'You don't understand. She's really ill. I need it all.'

Elizabeth narrowed her eyes, and ran a finger down the list. 'It won't come cheap.'

'I thought that... as they're for Abi...' I let my words hang.

'Oh no.' She slapped the list down on the table, and backed away, her hands up. 'You're asking me to give you all this for nothing? It's more than my job's worth. What would I say to Mr Jones?'

Her righteous expression riled me. I managed to hold myself in check, but only just. 'I'll pay,' I said, 'soon as I can. But it's all happened so quickly, I find myself temporarily... I mean if you could just wait a few days—'

Elizabeth gave a knowing smile. 'Mr Jones says not to give credit to the king's sympathisers.'

I felt rage rise in my throat. 'But it's for Abi. Surely you can make an exception? She can't come herself, and there's nobody else.'

'When we had bad harvests did the Fanshawes give us grain for nothing?'

'That was different. This is your own sister. Now, don't be a fool. Fetch me the things I need, for I'm not leaving without them. You owe it to Abi.'

'Fool am I? Don't take that tone with me. I've no need to do what you say. You don't own any of us anymore. Besides, I owe my sister nothing. Nothing!' Elizabeth stalked round the front of the table and stood before me, mouth set in a grim line. 'Do you know what she did? She burned down our house. Destroyed everything our parents had built, made us all paupers overnight. Why do you think my father turned to the liquor?'

'Now wait a minute—'

But she was in full spate, and she carried on shouting over me, 'I've clawed my way back up, and if there's one thing I've learnt through being poor, it's pride. Never to ask for credit. You think because you're the great Lady Katherine Fanshawe we'll all jump to serve you, but I'll tell you this – the king's gone. Fled, like the coward he is. Your title means nothing to us now; it's worthless. If you want anything from our shelves you'll have to pay on the nose, like everyone else in the village.'

The door behind Elizabeth opened and an elderly man with an eyeglass jammed in one eye, peered out, looking from one of us to the other.

'What's all this commotion?'

Elizabeth's face was red but she did not speak.

'I'm from the manor. I need these items straight away,' I said, with authority. I swept up the list from the table, and held it out to him. 'But I need them on tally.'

He plucked the eyeglass from his eye and stared at me. His eyes were cold and hard. 'Do you now? You'll not get a grain of dust from me. Even if you offered me a whole chest of bloody gold you'd not be welcome here. Your Royalist scum killed my son at Naseby.'

He turned and went back through the door. It shut behind him with a bang.

Elizabeth smirked, as if to say, 'Told you so,' as I backed away out of the shop. The venom in the man's eyes had pierced me like a dart. But that pain lasted only a moment. It was followed by incredulity. How could Elizabeth care so little for her own sister?

I burst back through the door. 'You don't deserve a sister!' I cried. 'If she dies,' I jabbed my finger at her, 'make no mistake – you will be responsible.'

The days were shorter now, and the sun was low and cold in the sky as I galloped home. I squinted through the rain, my hair whipping around my face, for the wind howled blustery from the north. My skirts soon grew sodden with wet. Poor Blaze – I cursed the weight of my woman's clothes and wished I was riding like a man again.

When I arrived, Mrs Binch was in the kitchen bending over a pot on the fire. She looked up hopefully as I arrived, but her face fell to see me empty handed. 'What happened?' she said, as my feet left wet footprints on the flags.

I told her.

Mrs Binch's face grew taut with outrage. 'The hussy. She wants a good slapping. If I ever get hold of her... what's the world coming to? What shall we do with no medicine? You'll have to go out, gather what you can from the hedgerows.'

'Me?'

'Yes. I can't ride, and you're not too grand to get a bit of mud on your hands are you?'

'It's not that. It's just... I don't know what to gather.'

Mrs Binch threw up her arms. 'Did no one teach you

anything?' Then her face softened. 'You're soaked. Come here by the fire.'

I warmed my wet hem by the embers.

'Abigail won't eat,' Mrs Binch said. 'I'm going to try her with some warm milk and honey from the hive. She's lost her fight. She won't open her eyes to me. And who can blame her, with so many of her family already in the ground? Except for her sisters. I suppose Martha's too small yet, to know what's happening. Has she heard anything from Elizabeth?'

'Not a word.'

Mrs Binch sniffed with disapproval, and picked up a ladle to stir the pot. 'I suppose Elizabeth refused to have Martha there, did she?'

'Weeks ago,' I said. 'She insisted there's more space here, which I suppose is true, but I can't help feeling she's loading all the responsibility onto Abi. It's just not fair, given that Elizabeth's the eldest.'

'Aye, she's always been a lazy sow. What will you do?'

'One good thing, I had a message from the parsonage yesterday; they'll keep Martha with them a while longer, until Abi is well again.'

'I can't believe Elizabeth and that Jones – that they'd have the gall to turn you away.'

'There's no welcome there.' I hitched my skirt and perched my hip on the edge of the table. 'I'm reaping the harvest of my stepfather and my husband. The tenants haven't forgotten Sir Simon's ruthless tithe collecting, nor Thomas, and how he danced to Sir Simon's tune. They remember there was no mercy from the Fanshawe men, not even in hard times.'

'This house needs life in it. I remember in your mother's time – so beautiful it was then, all the gentry from round about used to come for the big May ball. Lights twinkling in the chandeliers, the fires all lit, the ladies in their silks and satins. Then I really did have someone to cook for.' She paused to push me off the table. 'Look at it now, it's so sad, I don't know how you can bear to stay.'

'I know. But with my husband in exile, what choice do I have? I've no other relatives to take me in.'

There was no answer to that, so Mrs Binch pressed her hands on her back as if it ached. Then she sighed heavily and tipped the hot mixture into an earthenware cup. I passed her a cloth to wrap it in, and heard her boots creak up the stairs towards Abi's room.

I poked at the fire and it blazed up, so I backed away, watching steam wreathe from my skirt. In the old days, a chambermaid would have brought me a clean dry one, but no more. This last year had turned my life upside down. I was no longer the fine Lady Katherine Fanshawe, but just a girl, with a huge manor house to run.

4
TWO VISITORS

Next morning, the sound of a horse took me to the kitchen window. It darkened, then moments later Ralph's friend, Cutch, was at the door. He stood on the threshold, twisting his hat brim in his hands.

'Elizabeth says Abigail's ill,' he said.

'Where've you been?' My voice was sharper than I'd intended. 'Fine friend you are. You've been gone weeks, ever since the funeral, with never a word. We thought we'd seen the last of you.'

'Aye. Well I needed some time to think. Now Ralph's gone… well it hit me hard. I didn't want to be beholden.'

'You should've told us where you were—'

He held out a leather satchel. 'Never mind that now, I came to bring these.'

I sighed, and beckoned him in.

He dumped his bag on the table. 'It's a good thing I know a little about herbs,' he said, 'from the battlefield. There's rumours all over the village that Jones turned you away.'

'You gathered these?' Mistress Binch asked, pouncing on the bag. She picked through it. 'Shepherds' purse and feverfew.' Her face lit up in a smile. 'I can make a tisane.'

'Aye,' Cutch said. 'Mix it with honey. And there were late apples under the trees, and some plums. Oh, and I borrowed some oats.'

'Borrowed?' I raised my eyebrows.

'Soper's barn was open. His horses will have to go hungry.' Cutch nodded to Mrs Binch's face. 'That looks nasty. If you can spare a few, you could use some of these oats to make a poultice for that bruising.'

Mrs Binch raised her hand to her cheek. 'It's nothing. Better to eat it than waste good food.'

'Can I see Abi?' Cutch asked.

So it was, that Cutch came back into our lives. He never said where he'd been, but from the look of him, I could tell he'd been living rough. He had the same haunted look in his eyes as Abi.

When the drink was made, we went up to see her. The room was in semi-darkness, with just a wall sconce to illuminate the room. Even from the door we could hear her breath, rasping and shallow. Cutch was suddenly quiet. He tiptoed over, stared down at her. 'How long's she been ill like this?' he asked, his face angry.

'Five days? Six?' I couldn't be certain.

'And you only went to the apothecary yesterday?'

'We didn't think... I mean she just suddenly got worse, and I—'

'Hush! The last thing she needs is you two arguing.' Mrs Binch settled on the stool next to her, and tried to raise her up.

'She can't hear us,' I said, and Cutch glared at me.

'Here, let me help,' Cutch said, putting an arm under Abi's shoulders.

Abi felt us trying to move her and a spasm of coughing racked her. She opened her eyes briefly to look at Cutch but then turned over and twisted her head away from him.

He looked to me, hurt in his eyes.

Mrs Binch patted Abi's shoulder and tried to spoon some of

the liquid into Abi's mouth but it made her cough, and after that she kept her lips deliberately shut.

'We have to do something,' Cutch said, gripping the edges of his jerkin. 'She can't go on like this.'

'What?' I said. 'If she won't open her eyes to hear us, what can we do?'

'Enough. Get out, the pair of you.' Mrs Binch flapped a cloth at us. 'I dare say the horses want bedding down, and mistress, you could do worse than go and check the doors are locked. After that hold-up on the road, best not take chances.'

Cutch reluctantly went out. He took a last lingering look at Abi before he went. I followed him down the stairs, watched him slam out of the door and heard his boots crunch across the yard. I sighed with relief. He'd gone to the stable, and must be intending to stay. He'd sleep outside, in the hayloft, as he always did. He refused to sleep indoors in a bed – 'I've slept rough too many nights to change now,' he'd said.

Cutch was a conundrum. He took no wages and would not be ordered. Thomas, my husband, would have set such a rough fellow on the road straight away, but Cutch treated me like his equal. It was awkward not knowing what his station was. Was he a servant, or not? It was hard to know. But with him, I felt my ladylike upbringing and background more keenly than ever. Sometimes I thought him my friend, but sometimes I had the uncomfortable feeling he thought me a fool.

※

In the morning I was sick with grief again, vomiting into my chamber pot, and I dare not visit Abi for fear of giving her my contagion. Mrs Binch had stayed overnight, sleeping before the chamber fire in a chair dragged from the parlour. She said the herbs and potions were working. Abi's breathing had eased, and she coughed less. But still she kept her face turned to the wall, her eyes shut. She had refused to eat the barley mash I had made for her.

'She's wasting away,' Mrs Binch said.

Just at that moment, the back door creaked open and Cutch appeared with Martha clinging to his hand. I had only met Abi's sister once before, and it was a surprise to see this bonny six-year-old, cheeks rosy with cold, staring curiously up at me. In her hand hung a string from which dangled a turnip carved into a rough face.

'Look at my lantern,' she said.

'Did you make it?' asked Mrs Binch.

'Yes, all by myself,' she said. Then seeming to consider the truth of this, she pointed to Cutch. 'Except he helped.'

'It's very well done,' I said, but Martha interrupted me, 'It's for Abi. For All Hallows Eve.' She looked at Cutch with accusing eyes. 'You said Abi would be here. Where's Abi?'

'Upstairs,' I said. 'She's poorly.'

'Where?' Martha did not wait to be invited in, but ran off through the hall, then bounded up the stairs on her skinny legs and pushed open all the doors until she found the one with the shutters still closed. Cutch and I followed, hurrying to catch up with this whirlwind of flurrying skirts.

'Abi!' Martha ran and flung herself on the bed and began to shake her awake, bringing on a fresh bout of coughing. Martha made a face, and leapt back at the sudden noise.

'Come away now,' I said, beckoning from the door, fearful that Martha would make Abi worse. Abi propped herself up in bed, on weak elbows, 'No let her come.' Her voice was hoarse, barely a whisper, but just the sound of it made me want to leap with relief.

Martha pushed the lantern towards her and showed her the grinning face. 'For All Hallows Eve,' Martha said proudly, 'to keep the witches away.'

'Oh Martha,' Abi pulled her into an embrace, her shoulders shaking with sobs.

'Don't you like it?' Martha's face fell.

'It's beautiful. The best. The best I've ever seen.'

'Will you get up now, Abi? I've no one to play with. The vicar says Mother's gone to heaven. Will she come back for me? She took William and Ralph and I'm the one she left behind.'

'Leave Abi alone now,' I said. 'She's been very sick. But I think you made her feel better. Mrs Binch will be here soon and I think she could use a pair of hands like yours in the kitchen. I heard she might be making currant cakes. You can come back and see Abi again later.'

'Promise?'

'In a little while,' I said, 'when she's had more rest.'

'Cutch!' Martha tugged at his sleeve. 'Piggyback? Please?'

Cutch hoisted Martha onto his back and held onto her arms as she wrapped her legs round him. He pretended to neigh. Martha giggled and slapped at him to make him go faster. Abi followed their gallop round the room with her eyes, until they galumphed away down the stairs. My queasiness forgotten, I went to her. A wan smile curved her lips, and it gladdened my heart.

I knelt and leaned against the bed, mouthed, 'About time too. You've been sleeping for days.'

'How long?'

She was looking at me. Praise God. I held up seven fingers. 'A week? More. We feared for you, thought you might...'

'I didn't want to wake up. I can't believe they won't come back. Why, Kate? Why my family? Do you think it's because I burned down our house? I never meant to.'

'No, I'm sure—'

'I was just careless with the candle. It was an accident. Do you think God's still punishing me? With my deafness, I thought I'd paid that debt already.'

'Don't talk of debts. It's nonsense.' God's reasoning was beyond me.

'Ralph had promised to give Mr Mallinson my dowry. Now he's gone, there'll be no one to find me a marriage portion. Jacob might not want me, and then what will I do?' She paused as another cough rattled her chest. 'And someone has to look after Martha. Jacob won't want to take on Martha too.' She coughed again, eyes filled with tears.

I passed her my kerchief. 'He'll think of something. Don't worry.'

She sank back a little. 'But what will happen to us when Thomas takes you away to France?'

'I'm going nowhere. I've heard not a word from him. Maybe he won't send for me. Lie back now, and I'll bring you some more of Mrs Binch's tisane.'

'But at the burials there was all this talk of closing up the house. It was on everyone's lips. Constable Mallinson says the County Sequestration Committee is to decide soon—'

'Hush. Enough talking. Rest.' I had not been privy to the gossip of them closing up the house. It made me bitter, that it was my inheritance, my dwelling house, yet I would be the last to know its fate. Abi had voiced my own fears and they rankled.

But the civil wars had done some good – my stepfather had gone, and my weakling husband was missing. For the first time in my life I could order my own fate. And I wasn't going to give up that privilege easily. I would not be blown by the wind. I would carve out my own future, somehow.

※

The next morning Abi was a little better, and I hurried to answer the hammering at the door. Jacob Mallinson was standing on the doorstep. He was immaculately dressed in a dark twill doublet and breeches, his dark hair combed away from his face. He looked more the gentleman than ever. It made me edgy, as I was still clad in an old smoke-stained apron and coif. He held a big pannier in his arms which he offered to me.

'Morrow, Kate,' he said, his breath steaming in the chill air. 'Elizabeth told me that Abigail is unwell. I've brought her some remedies. I asked Elizabeth what she might need and she was so helpful.'

I'll wager she was, I thought grimly, *as long as it was you that was asking, and not me.* But I kept these thoughts to myself. 'You'd best come in,' I said.

In the background I saw Cutch's face darken. He turned away and led Jacob's horse to the trough.

'How is she?' Jacob asked, removing his hat.

'A little better, but weak. But I'll fetch Mrs Binch, and let's see what she can do with what you've brought. If you wait a moment, I'll fetch my purse and—'

'No need. It's a gift. My pleasure.'

I exhaled. My purse was empty, but I would not let Jacob know that. Though as soon as he stepped over the threshold, I immediately felt the paucity of our surroundings. Before Thomas had left, he had replaced some of our furniture, but not all. Some rooms were uncomfortably empty, with telltale pale squares where our family portraits used to grace the walls. I pushed these thoughts away.

'Would you like to come up and see her?' Perhaps it was what Abi needed, to see Jacob. It might give her another reason to get well.

I gestured to him to follow, but I sensed some reluctance, a hanging back. 'Sorry Kate, but I'm not good with sick people,' he said, with a grimace. 'You can tell her I called, though.'

'It's Abi,' I said, 'not just anyone. And she'll want to see you.' I set off upstairs, so he had to follow. I glanced back to see him running a hand round the inside of his stock to loosen it. I took him to where Mrs Binch was bent over, one hand on Abi's shoulder.

'Ssh,' she said, looking up. 'Don't wake her.'

'Come and sit by her,' I said, beckoning to Jacob.

He perched himself on the stool that Mrs Binch had just vacated, looking uncomfortably stiff in his starched cravat and fine doublet. I saw him cast a horrified glance to Mrs Binch's bruised face, before his attention went back to Abi. 'Is it catching?' he whispered to Mrs Binch.

'No,' she reassured him. 'At least nobody else has shown any signs of ailing. Why don't you hold her hand?'

Jacob stretched out his hand and took hold of Abi's but he did not seem to know what to do with it. He held it gingerly, as though it might bite him. Abi was sound asleep; her face was pale, her breath laboured.

Suddenly, she coughed and opened her eyes. Seeing Jacob she shut them again tight.

'Talk to her,' I said, in desperation. 'Tell her she's to get well. That we all need her.'

'Can she hear me?'

'Of course she can't hear you! But you need to tell her through your touch.'

He squeezed her hand. 'Your sister sends her best wishes. She sent you some potions from the apothecary.'

'Don't suppose she said she'd visit, though,' I muttered.

'You'll soon be up and about,' Jacob continued lamely. He seemed unable to imagine how to talk to her without using words. Abi turned over, dragging the blanket over her head.

Jacob sighed, and stood up. I did not like the way he rubbed his own hand on his breeches as if it was contaminated. 'Can I speak to you in private a moment,' he said.

I let him follow me out onto the landing.

'There was a coach held up two nights ago on the main London road, that's why I haven't been before. We've been too busy. Two of Cromwell's right-hand men were shot dead by highway thieves on the way to London, and their coach was stolen too. It's a big investigation.' His face glowed with enthusiasm. 'Father and I are working on it together. You need to lock your doors and—'

'I know,' I said. I told him in whispers about how we had been held up by the two men.

'You were robbed? Why did I not know of this? What did they take?'

I did not want to tell him the humiliation of being stripped to my shift. 'Nothing,' I said. 'We had no valuables with us, and they hit Mrs Binch when they found no gold. Then they let us go. They saw the other coach coming, and lost interest in us. We heard shots, but we didn't stop, we just wanted to get ourselves away.'

'But you should have told us.' His brown eyes held a hint of accusation. 'We could have been hot on their trail! Why didn't you come for the constable?'

'Keep your voice down. I'll tell you why – because Abi was all alone here and ill, and I feared she might die if I did not get home soon.'

'We could have caught them,' Jacob insisted. 'Can you describe them?'

'Would you have left Abi all alone in this big house with no one to look to her?'

'Well no, of course not.' He frowned. 'I shall expect you to come over later and tell me a full description of these men. Lock all your doors, and make sure no one travels without an escort.'

'Oh we will,' I said as we went back down. 'As you can see, the house is full of people waiting to escort us.' I gestured bitterly at the bare walls and empty hall.

As Jacob reached the door and swung it open, he suddenly turned. 'My father and I have been talking and we wondered…

what will happen to Abi, when you... if you have to leave here? I don't think we can—'

'What do you mean?' My heart had turned to ice. He was the second person to talk of me leaving.

'Father's on the sequestration committee. They're deciding what to do about the manor. It seems you have few friends in the neighbourhood. It doesn't look good for the Fanshawes, not when there's talk of enforced sales of Royalist houses – to raise money to rebuild in St Albans.'

'Who said this? Who's making these decisions?'

'The Justice of the Peace, Hodgson. And my father of course, as he's responsible for law and order. One or two others too, like myself and Jack Downall.'

A draught blew in from the door, chill as winter. Downall. I did not want to hear that name again.

Jacob put his hand on my arm. 'I know you don't like him, but your stepfather approves. I guess he sees the advantages of appearing sympathetic to Cromwell's views.'

'Downall's only after lining his own pockets. He'd be on the side of the devil if it paid him.'

'Hodgson's a staunch Puritan, and Downall's made a friend of him. I must warn you that he's fuelling the fire that you're a nest of papists here and—'

'Papists? Don't talk such foolishness. You know that to be false.' I cut him off. My heart had turned into a knot of tension in my chest. This was real. My husband was missing. Without the house I would have no inheritance, no stake in my own future. I drew myself up. 'When do this committee meet?'

'They won't see you.' He'd read my mind.

'Why not? Downall is a bully and a liar. He changes sides so quickly you can't see him for dust. They'll see me. I'll make them.'

'You won't. Because you're a woman. Women aren't allowed in these meetings, they get too emotional.'

'Is that what *you* think?' I was on fire with anger, I advanced on him so he backed away.

'No.' He held up his hands. 'Of course not. But it's the way the law works. You have to follow along with it, not stir up more heat.'

'I thought you were my friend, Jacob.'

'I am. Any good friend would give you the same advice. The Royalists have lost. In your position I'd be humble. Stay in line, don't upset the apple cart. Wait for the wheel of fortune to swing round.'

'It's fine for you to talk, from your perch as constable's boot boy, laying down the law, with no one to answer to except your father.'

I'd insulted him. His face grew rigid and he placed his hat firmly back on his head.

'Take care, Kate. You've enemies enough.' He walked to the stable where Cutch was standing holding his horse. Cutch got no thanks, but stood back as Jacob dug his heels into his horse's flanks and galloped away, divots of mud flying back from his horse's hooves.

I held up my hands in a hopeless gesture of frustration. What had I done? Abi was only just coming back to health, but she'd turn round and die if she knew Jacob had galloped away in such a temper.

※

Back in the bedchamber, Abi sat up in a welter of coughing. 'Why did you have to let him in? Look at me, I'm not fit to be seen.'

'I thought it would cheer you, to see him.'

'Like this? In a sweat-soaked chemise with my hair all in rats' tails? How could you?' She scrubbed away an angry tear.

'He was pleased to see you getting better.'

'Rot. It was so embarrassing. You should've waited until...' Coughing prevented her from finishing.

I tried to hand her a drink but she pushed it away so it slopped over my wrist. 'Just go away. I don't want you here.'

'I was only trying to help. And I'll have you remember, this is my house, and I'll go where I please.'

I slammed the door on the way out.

Immediately I regretted it. I took a candle and wandered the empty rooms. There was an ache in my heart from Abi's harsh words, but I wasn't going to let her see how much it hurt. I had so few friends, I realised. I hadn't been allowed the easy camaraderie of the children on the village green. I remembered Ralph's words, that wealth could be a blessing or a curse.

I walked along the long echoing gallery where portraits of my forebears had once gazed coolly from their frames, past the library, now empty of books, into the sitting room where now only two chairs stood like islands in a sea of space.

This was all I had. In a sense, the house *was* me. At my stepfather's insistence, Thomas had married the house and my inheritance, caring nothing for me as a person. Fate had stripped the manor of its assets, and now even Thomas had run away from it. I ran my hand over one of the chairs and rubbed the silt of dust between my fingers.

A shadow passed across the wall, fleeting, like a bird flying past the window. The movement was disturbing in this quiet room. I could not help but turn, but I knew before I even looked, that the room would be empty.

'*A blessing,*' Ralph's voice whispered inside my head, '*or a curse.*'

5
A GRAND VISION

ALL HALLOWS EVE, and Abi was much better, sitting up in bed now, but thin as a lath. Jacob had not found time to visit, and nor had Abi's sister Elizabeth, but Mrs Binch had come every day.

'She's perked up no end,' Mrs Binch said. 'It's a world of difference since I came last.'

'It was seeing Martha,' I said. 'Cutch brought her. But Abi wants her here – she can't stay at the vicarage for ever, and Elizabeth – well, she's not very motherly.'

Mrs Binch gave a snort of disgust. 'She's not worth your breath, you mean. Fancy her not showing her face at all. I thought poor Abigail wasn't going to make it, she'd lost the will to fight.'

'Too much grief, in too short a time.'

'You too, mistress, if you don't mind me saying. There's something... I don't know, different about you.'

I tossed my head, ignored it. If there was one thing I could not bear it was folk feeling sorry for me. I changed the subject. 'Mrs Binch, is there any chance you could stay on? I can't offer you much in the way of wages, but the house needs more managing, and I can't do it alone. I need a live-in housekeeper.'

'Are you offering it to me? A housekeeper's position?'

'I can't think of anyone else I'd trust.'

'But there's no servants for me to manage! This house has had its day. They say in the village it will be taken over by one of Cromwell's Roundheads, so it's only a matter of time. Me, a housekeeper? What a cockeyed notion!'

'It won't always be like this. I've an idea to turn it around. Will you take time to think about it?'

'No. What can you do? A young girl like you? Besides, I know my mind. And I like my own bed at night. I'm very flattered I'm sure, but there's too many ghosts walk this place after dark.' She shivered, looked over her shoulder. 'I'll take my own cottage, thanks all the same.'

That night I lit the turnip lantern and it stood in Abi's chamber, its gap-toothed grin a warning to anything outside the walls. All Hallow's Eve, when the veil between the worlds was at its thinnest. I was glad to know Cutch was out there in the stables.

Abi was still recovering, and though she had been up and out of bed to wash, and to mend her patched apron, she was still too weak to do much. I sat in a chair in her room, where the fire was lit, and finished off her mending. My stitches were clumsy; I was unused to such work, and the light was bad.

I told myself I was not afraid of witches, but I hung bay leaves in the window just the same.

The wind had grown wilder and now it whistled through the trees at the edge of the fields; leaves blew past the windows. I heard a stable door bang, and it made me leap from my seat. *Only the wind*, I thought, *or Cutch bedding down the horses.*

I was just nipping off the thread with my teeth when I heard hoof beats. At first I thought it was my imagination, but then came the unmistakeable clatter of iron shoes in the yard. I ran to the hall window and looked out to see three horses. Three cloaked men, their hats hanging down their backs, hair whipping round their heads with the wind. Cutch appeared in the yard to speak to them. I saw him shake his head as if he wanted them to leave, but moments later, there was a thudding at the door.

'Who is it?' I called, searching frantically for a weapon, but there was nothing close by.

'Constable Mallinson,' came the reply.

Jacob's father. What could he want, riding out after dark on a night such as this?

'A moment,' I called. I tucked my hair into a knot at the nape of my neck, unpinned my apron, before smoothing down my taffeta skirts.

When I opened the door the first face I saw was Downall. It was as if I'd been punched in the guts. I took an involuntary step back. Constable Mallinson took this as an invitation and the three men pushed their way into the hall. Jacob Mallinson followed just behind his father. They filled the space making me back away down to the parlour. Hastily, hands shaking, I lit a wall sconce, and a candelabra.

Last time I saw Downall he had tried to storm the house with his frenzied Puritan mob, and Ralph had narrowly escaped a hanging. Downall's jowly face filled me with hatred, a venom black as gall. I was grateful to see Cutch follow the men into the parlour. I nodded to him, to indicate he should stay.

Mallinson pointed me to a chair but I did not sit. 'Jacob says you were held up last week by thieves,' Mallinson said. 'We're here to get a description.'

'It's too late for such business,' I said. 'Come again in the morning.'

'We will not take much time, and we need your testimony,' Jacob said. 'The dead men were important men. It won't wait.'

'I'll talk to you and your father, Jacob, but I refuse to talk to a man who only a few months ago broke down my front door.' I restrained myself, but glared in Downall's direction. I couldn't bear to look at him. Was it only I who saw the carefully veiled threat in his eyes?

'You've no choice,' Mallinson said, 'or you'll be obstructing the course of justice.'

'A night in the cell would not be pleasant,' Downall said, glancing at me sidelong. He'd removed his hat, and his sandy hair was flattened to his head.

'You can't arrest her, she's done nothing wrong,' Cutch said. 'She said, she'll speak to the constable, not to you.'

'I don't know what business it is of yours, but I'm acting as assistant to Mr Mallinson,' Downall said.

'On the contrary,' Cutch stuck out his chin, 'I don't know what business it is of yours.'

'Downall's presence here is quite legitimate,' Mallinson said in a placatory tone.

'For your information,' Downall said, puffing out his chest, 'Cromwell appointed me as one of his county representatives to ensure Puritan rule is followed to the letter. And that includes making sure felons are brought to justice.'

Mallinson unrolled parchment onto the table and weighted it with four lead weights. 'Please bear with us. We're only following instructions from the Protectorate.' He passed me a quill and uncorked the ink. 'Now Mistress Fanshawe, write down what you remember,' he said. His words had a calculated finality about them. For the first time I saw Mallinson the constable, instead of Mallinson, Jacob's father.

'If I do this, will he leave?'

Mr Mallinson glanced at Downall, who inclined his head. So the constable's still in that bastard's pocket after all, I thought. So much for the laws of England.

I wrote all I could remember. Part of me wanted to resist, but the other part of me remembered how the highwayman had hit Mrs Binch across the face. That man should pay the price. I could not give much of a description, because it had been dark and the whole event had a strange unreality about it. The shock, I suppose. And the blood-stopping sounds of those shots. I could only remember the hard expression in the short man's eyes, the skirt pooling at my feet, the sudden draught as the tree crashed down.

When I'd done, Downall snatched up the parchment and took it immediately under the sconce where he frowned over it for a good few minutes. He waved it dismissively. 'Just like the old woman,' he said. 'She can't help us.'

'You talked to Mrs Binch?' I asked.

'Last night. She couldn't give us a good description either,' Jacob said.

'Said it was too dark to see anything,' Downall said. 'Strange, that.'

Something about his watchful demeanour made me even more alert.

He pressed his hat back on his head. 'Let's away,' he said. 'We have what we need.'

And in a flurry of cloaks and clanking of swords they were out of the house just as quickly as they had come.

※

When they'd gone I slumped into a chair. Their questions had drained me. I did not know what to do. Downall had Constable Mallinson under his thumb. With no men here to protect us, and no other servants, Abi and I were vulnerable, and I felt our frailty. But what to do? Even Mrs Binch refused to stay. Somehow, I would have to make my own community

Ralph, what would you do? The thought was not quite a prayer. Almost immediately an answer came back, *Barton and Whistler.* The thought was clear as a spring, as if Ralph himself had spoken. The Diggers.

A tingling sensation, and the room suddenly fell to absolute silence. I searched for his presence, but could feel only my own heartbeat in the cave-like darkness of the room.

Suddenly the vision opened up before me. The house was big enough for all of us. All I had to do was share it. I couldn't pay wages, but I could provide shelter and a roof over their heads, and land to till. And we'd be like a village unto ourselves; that way we could support each other and thrive. No more building wattle houses on the common land where they would be torn down, but each person could have their own place here.

It was what I'd promised Ralph, without even realising it. That we would build the Diggers' dream right here at Markyate Manor.

I stood and walked to look out at the thin sliver of moon hovering over the misty lawn. The idea felt perfect. Ralph would have loved it. The fact that he would not be here to see it come to fruition brought tears to my eyes.

Of course it would be a risk. My menfolk might return from exile, and Sir Simon Fanshawe would rather see me horse-whipped in hell, than see our land turned over to the Diggers.

I paced and paced, weighing the decision. Now was not the best time, for winter was already reaching its chill frost over the land like a creeping beast. But I couldn't sit here a moment longer and do nothing, with this empty useless shell of a house weighing on my shoulders, and the fields falling fallow for lack of care.

I'd turn this house round, fill it with life and laughter. Build something lasting, in memory of Ralph.

6

A CHILL IN THE HEART

THE NEXT DAY Abi tottered to breakfast holding Martha's hand in hers. She propped a sack of meal on the chair for Martha to sit on so she could reach to eat her curds and bread. Abi's face was still grey and her eyes red rimmed. She did not eat, and I wished she would; her wrists looked all bone.

'Here,' I said, pushing over the loaf and the butter crock.

'I'm not hungry,' she said, avoiding my eye, passing Martha a damp cloth to wipe her hands.

I tapped her on the shoulder so she was forced to look up. 'I know. The thought of food makes me ill too, but we must eat. Will you help me clean the top bedrooms? I'm going to see if the Diggers want to build their community here.'

She shook her head. 'Here? You mean in the house?'

'Yes. We've too much space here. Why not share it?'

'What about your husband?'

Husband. Strange word for such a gangling youth. I had no feeling for him, could not imagine loving any other boy but Ralph. Ralph, with his strong muscled arms, his eyes blue as cornflowers. More alive than Thomas, even in death, even in my memory.

'Thomas has gone,' I said, 'and I've had no word. So he won't know. And in any case, he's too frightened of Downall and the villagers, of what they'll do to Royalists like him, to come back. I hope I never see him again.'

'Oh Kate, you fool,' she whispered. Her eyes had turned glassy. 'Can you not choose an easier path?'

'Don't you see? It's what Ralph would have wanted.'

'But it's begging for trouble. Why not lay low for a while, keep quiet? Bow to Cromwell's ideas? It's foolish to do anything to rouse folks' temper. At the funeral, Jacob told me we're best to keep ourselves to ourselves. If you do such a thing, it will only cause talk in the village.'

'It's my land, and it's what I promised to Ralph.'

'They said Ralfie won't come back,' Martha began to cry, as if she'd only just realised he'd gone.

Abi turned to her, with that sixth sense she always seemed to have as far as Martha was concerned. 'Hush, peachkins, let's finish this bread. Eat it all up, then we'll go and see if Cutch can make you a little loom, and you can try some weaving.'

'I don't want to ... want to go home ... want Mama.' Martha began to bawl in earnest. Abi picked her up and held her, but she kicked and screamed to get down, and in the end it made Abi cough, and she had to let go.

Abi slumped into a chair, head in her hands. 'How can I tell her they're gone, so she'll understand?' I shook my head. Death was too hard a conundrum, even for me.

'What's all this?' Cutch appeared at the kitchen door just in time to scoop Martha up. 'Jiggedy, jiggedy, my fine horse,' he said jogging her up and down, and with a big swoop, he pretended to drop her.

Half-terrified, half-elated, Martha was soon demanding, 'Do it again!'

Cutch galloped her outside piggyback and shouting for more.

How quickly her temper changed, and how quickly her tears were forgotten. Would that it were like that for me.

❦

Despite Abi's misgivings, I sent word to Barton and Whistler to ask them to come up to the house. I was restless, filled with enthusiasm for my new idea. In the end, it was a good thing I sent Cutch because when he got back he told me they were reluctant, and he didn't think they'd come.

'But why? Surely they can see the sense of it – that they will have a share in all this?' I gestured expansively at the lawns outside the window.

'You're too young. They don't trust you.'

'Then I'll make them. Once they find they are housed in fine big rooms, and that they have all these acres to work, they'll come round. I know they will.'

Cutch made a grimace, and went back to the stables.

His words made me nervous. Sure enough, when Barton and Whistler arrived they stood uncomfortably in the big parlour whilst I explained. I remembered them building their shanty houses on the common. There, they had looked purposeful and tough, like wild horses. In here, they seemed to shrink. They shuffled from foot to foot, not looking into my eyes.

I asked them where they were living now, and Barton rubbed his beard and said he was living in shared rooms above the inn.

'I'm not sure,' he said. 'What about Mother?'

'Bring her,' I said. 'Bring them all. Whoever wants to come.'

Barton and Whistler looked at each other as if they could not believe it.

'Anyone with Ralph's principles is welcome here.' I drew back my shoulders, tried to hide my disappointment at their lack of enthusiasm. I had looked up to Whistler, thought to impress him.

'It's backwards,' Whistler said. 'The likes of us, in this grand house. And your husband will not like it.'

'He's not here,' I said tartly.

'I don't know. It's one thing building on common land, another moving into this... this place,' Whistler said. 'It wasn't what Winstanley had in mind. He said we'd to live simply.'

'It's just brick and mortar. What use is it lying empty? And there's enough room for us all. Do it for Ralph, if not for me. Winstanley hated waste, did he not? Well, my land is growing thick with weed and bramble, no crops have been sown for the spring. There is enough land here to support us all, and in hard times, we can help each other.'

'But you're just a girl—' Barton said.

'A girl with seventy acres.'

They looked to one another again. 'How many of us can you take?' Barton asked.

'As many as you like. Ask your wives. They'd surely see the sense in it.'

Whistler shuffled, uncertain, and from the corner of my eye I caught Barton shaking his head.

I shot him a purposeful look. 'Do you not remember the song? *Stand up now, Diggers all*. If Ralph were here, he'd tell you, you'd be fools not to try it.'

Barton raised his chin. 'If Ralph were here, he'd have thought it a damn fool idea.'

※

But they must have talked it over because a few days later the kitchen door never stopped opening and closing. Though I had told the Diggers they could come in through the front door, none of them could believe it, and they all, to a one, used the tradesman's entrance. With them they brought their few possessions, the richest of which was a sack of bruised corn and an elderly cow, still in milk.

Susan, Owen Whistler's wife, was amazed when I showed her the bedroom she was to sleep in. Of course it was unfurnished, but her eyes were wide as trenchers, 'By heaven, it's as big as a house! And this just for me and Owen and the little ones?'

'I've plenty of room. Do with it what you will. If you need wood for the fire, take some. We'll arrange how to restock it later. It won't be too hard to scour the forest if we work together.'

'Thank you milady, it's more than—'

I held up my hand, pleased to feel a benefactor again. 'No, don't thank me. You will work for it. We all will. And it can be plain Kate. No titles here, remember.'

I left her unrolling her straw palliasse and staring around.

By supper time twenty-five people had moved into the house, and the refectory table in the dining hall was full for the first time in almost a year. There were not enough stools, so Cutch had made benches by standing planks on empty barrels. A fire roared in the hearth, and Susan, Margery and the other women had produced a pigeon stew. Spirits were high.

'Let us say grace,' said Whistler. To my pleasure, he gave thanks for my generosity and prayed for God's guidance over the coming labours. We all said a fervent 'Amen'.

The only quiet people at the table were Abi and Cutch. Abi always struggled to follow conversations when many were talking, because she did not know who to lip-read. And she kept a wary eye on little Martha, who was pink-cheeked with excitement, having more children to keep her company. Soon she and little Jonty Barton were playing a game with a wooden ball under the table.

Cutch was too quiet. I could see him weighing up the men as potential adversaries. I suppose that's what being a soldier does for you, and he was still worried for Abi. He kept glancing her way. He was on guard, I realised; he trusted no one, not even the Diggers.

The next day the men began to plough, though it was late to do so, and we had no heavy horses. The men had to furrow and till the earth by hand, and it was hard work. Cutch offered to help and to oil up rusty plough blades. The weather was windy and the rain lashed down, but we women worked hard to churn butter from Susan's cow, and to grind our meagre supply of corn into flour. There was not much food to feed us all, but by sharing we had more than we could have managed alone.

For a few weeks things went well. My grief had become a dull ache, I was no longer physically sick with it, and the fact I was doing something useful in Ralph's memory eased the gnawing pain I carried for him. But then the weather worsened and the land, being flat, became waterlogged, making the men's work harder. Small grumbles became bigger grumbles, and what had seemed like minor problems became big concerns.

The fields were more mud than grass now, and through lack of nourishment the elderly cow had stopped giving milk. One day the men brought in the bloodied carcass of the cow and we had to salt it in a barrel, and smoke it, boil jelly from the hooves and cook up the innards.

Never had I done such a thing before. The stink of blood and bone made my gorge rise. Margery Barton watched my white face with an expression of glee, passing me the slotted spoon to stir the congealing mass over the big fire in the copper pan. We hung the flanks of the carcass in the outside buttery when it was done, to keep them cold, but the meat did not last long. She was a scrawny beast, and there were too many mouths to feed.

One morning, a few weeks later, we awoke to find the last flank of beef had gone. It had been stolen in the night. Nobody had heard anything, not even Cutch, who slept in the stables, but it made me wish we had a couple of dogs. I did not like the idea of strangers sneaking about our yard. It brought me in mind of the highwaymen. I looked at the empty hook where the meat had hung, and shuddered.

Our pooled supplies soon ran out. None of us had any money. We debated what to sell, and finally settled on the spare harness in the tack room. Cutch was sent into the village with Abi's pony, Pepper, and the cart to sell it.

He returned disheartened, with the saddlery still in the cart. 'They would not buy,' he said. 'They know I'm from the manor. I tried Soper at the hiring yard, and he said nobody would touch anything from the manor. It brings bad luck, he said. They believe you are cursed, that you bring death to those you are close to.'

My heart sank. 'Did you try the blacksmiths?' I asked.

'Same story. Except he was even more insulting. Said he'd heard rumours you were housing dissenters, and he wants nothing to do with us. It's not good news. He said Downall's already put in a report to the Protectorate to suggest you should be stopped.'

'Oh Lord. I thought with more of us, it might persuade them, that they would trade with us.'

'No. Banding together's made it worse. They see you as a real threat now to their Puritan order. Cromwell always spat on the Levellers and the Diggers – thought they divided his army. He liked them even less than the Royalists. Don't suppose his opinion has changed much, either.'

'What do you suggest, then? Try St Albans?'

Cutch sighed. 'Don't know. It's a fair ride over there, and daylight's short this time of year. But we must feed people, or they can't work. I've no easy answers. Maybe someone else has. We should ask them. Tonight over supper.'

Supper was a thin soup of barley and root vegetables. I was

hungry. All at once, from being too grief-stricken to hold anything down, I craved something to fill my belly.

Abi read my thoughts, as I surveyed my empty bowl. 'Sorry, Kate. There wasn't much left to make a meal.'

'Aye, the last of the leeks came up today, and the clamping pit for the winter parsnips is empty,' Whistler said. 'We've just eaten the last of them. Don't know what we'll do now. We sowed chard, but the rain's washed it out. Wasted all that work. And another thing – the temperature's dropped. Reckon we might have another frost tonight.'

'We're out of wood for burning too,' Margery said. 'We can't cook without wood.'

'We gathered what we could, but it will be too damp to burn for a fortnight,' Barton said. His depressed manner irritated me.

'No need to get downhearted,' I said. 'At least you've shelter, and land to plough and sow. More than some folks.' I tried not to make this sound pointed, but a few of the men frowned. I tried to rescue it, 'Maybe it is hard right now, but it will come right for us if we just persevere. We should ask God for his guidance.'

'It's hard not being able to trade,' Whistler grumbled. 'And that's because you're not well liked.'

'It is none of my doing,' I said. 'It was ever so for the Diggers. We shouldn't have to rely on trade. We should be sufficient unto ourselves, isn't that what Winstanley said?'

'Ah, but he gave it up as unworkable. So's everyone else,' Whistler said. 'We're the only ones left.'

'All the more reason to stick to it then,' I said.

At this everyone stared glumly at their empty plates. Except for me, not one of the women had spoken; all had let their menfolk talk for them. So much for Winstanley's ideas of women being equal to men. I wondered though if it was the fact of my class that made me confident to speak. Had I been a serving woman by birth, would I have been so outspoken? Clearly this idea of living in community was harder than I had imagined.

Nobody had an answer, and in the end we women took away the dishes to wash, and asked the men to leave their boots in the kitchen to be cleaned. As I chipped mud off Whistler's boots, and cursed him for his miserable attitude, I wondered if I had done the right thing inviting this ungrateful horde into my house.

That night I dreamt Ralph stood before me, in his doeskin breeches and brown twill doublet, standing in the middle of the room, his hair even blonder in the candlelight. I cried out, and took a step back. Even dreaming, I knew him to be a phantom, yet he appeared so real.

For a moment I could not move, my hand was clasped to my throat. 'Ralph?'

He did not answer, or maybe he could not. He gazed at me with such love, his eyes soft pools of brown, shadowed by pain. He was still, just staring down at me.

'Ralph, I need you...' In my dream I walked towards him to feel his arms circle me, to take comfort, but as soon as I moved he began to fade, like the mist when the sun comes out. My ears buzzed, my skin prickled. I reached out a hand, but it touched empty air. I was too late. He was gone. I cried out for him again.

Abi clambered out of her truckle bed and went downstairs. A few moments later she returned, passing me a hot posset.

'Drink,' she said. 'All this, filling the house with strangers – it won't bring him back, you know,' she said.

'I see him sometimes,' I said.

She shook her head.

'You don't believe me, do you?' I said.

'I don't know what to believe. I just know that it's eating you up, that you are always looking over your shoulder. And he's dead, Kate. He's not coming back.'

'I saw him. Under the old oak.'

Abi sighed, her face resigned, eyes dark shadows. 'You have to let him go, Kate.'

'You think I'm losing my wits, don't you?'

'No, no. But it worries me. It's not healthy. It's as if you can't settle to anything. This wild idea with the Diggers—'

'No!' I stood up. 'It's you who can't settle. You used to be the hardest worker I know, but these last weeks, nothing has been done. Look at the place – the fires upstairs are cold, dust lies over everything.' I saw her face tighten with indignation, but I couldn't stop my mouth, though I knew it was hurting her. 'The sheets are damp on the beds, my laundry basket is overflowing.'

'I've been ill. What do you expect? And I miss him too you know. He was my brother.' Abi's voice cracked.

I took a sip of the posset, but it was still too hot, and my hand was shaking. I pushed it away.

Abi stood up in one quick movement, and grabbed the cup, thrusting it towards me so it spilled over the lip and onto the coverlet. 'You'll drink it, if I have to pour it down your throat! Do you think it's easy for me? To wait on you here of all places? Well do you? My brother murdered up there in that bedroom?'

'Don't shout, you'll wake Martha.'

'And haven't you noticed, there's been no sign of Jacob. Not hide not hair of him. He's not been near us for nigh on a month.'

'I hadn't—'

'You've never noticed. You've never even asked after him. You're so self-obsessed you haven't even thought how I might be feeling…' She stopped. Closed her mouth tight shut, as if she had suddenly realised she was my servant, not my friend. 'I'm sorry. I'm just tired. Tired of being alive when the rest of my family…' A sob, and she turned without a word, grabbed the rushlight from the wall sconce and left me. Her footsteps echoed away, down the broad sweeping stairway, down the stone kitchen steps to the kitchen.

I drank the posset though it made me gag. She was right. I was immediately sorry. I hadn't thought of her enough. Her loss was as great as mine – worse, for she had lost her mother to the vengeful Copthorne, as well as her brother Ralph. My Ralph.

And now she mentioned it, she was right. I'd been so busy I'd forgotten Jacob. Though Abi had always seemed tough on the outside, I sensed the insecurity in her that deafness brought. Her mother used to push her forward, make her do more than she thought she could, but she was gone. And now it looked like she'd lost Jacob too, and I knew how painful that must feel. I hadn't meant to hurt her, but somehow I seemed to be better at losing friends than keeping them.

※

The next morning I'd no time to find Abi before there was a rap at the door, and a messenger on horseback bringing me a letter. The cold red wax bore the imprint of the Fanshawe fleur-de-lis. It was addressed in Sir Simon's florid, cursive hand to my husband, Thomas. I took it to my chamber, my throat suddenly tight with anxiety. If Sir Simon was writing to Thomas here, then Thomas obviously had not yet reached my stepfather in exile.

But it had been months. If Thomas had not got to France, what had become of him? My mind rushed through the possibilities. I could not help but hope he'd met some ill fortune on the way.

I rushed downstairs to find Abi, and took her to one side to show her the letter. 'What should I do?'

She was somewhat cool with me. 'What you wish.'

'I'm asking your advice.'

'The letter must have taken weeks to get here, and Thomas has probably got to Sir Simon in France by now. Just put it to one side.' Her look was a warning, she saw I was in mind to open it, and because I knew she'd disapprove, I left it.

Over the next few days it sat there, like an accusation. The presence of this letter was highly disturbing, almost as if my stepfather himself were in the room. He would not approve of my 'lodgers', this I knew. I hoped word would not get back to him, but I assumed that he would not return to bother us whilst ever he was on Cromwell's list of undesirables. The letter reminded me I was treading a thin line, one over a chasm that could finish me for good.

Over the next weeks more letters came with Sir Simon's seal, until finally a letter came addressed to me. The fact that Sir Simon should consider writing to me at all was a wonder.

Katherine,

Is Thomas ill? He has not replied to my letters. Are they reaching you? If so, why no reply? Please write and advise me at the earliest convenience. S.F.

His usual rudeness. Not a 'how are you?' or a greeting. I wrote a curt letter back explaining that Thomas had fled after a disturbance in the village and was on his way to him in France. I had not seen Thomas since September. I thought of him, out somewhere in this freezing weather, and could not help but wonder what had become of him. I was sorry for him. He had always seemed so weak, caught under his uncle's thumb. Besides, I had no love for him, Ralph consumed all my love. Even now Ralph was gone, not an hour went by that I did not think of him.

But two weeks later another letter with the Fanshawe seal arrived, again addressed to me.

My stepfather wanted to make enquiries about his nephew. He was coming home to Markyate Manor.

7
THE DANGERS OF SNOW

I SLEPT BADLY, wondering how on earth I could explain the Digger community to my stepfather. Sir Simon must be mighty keen to find Thomas to risk coming back here into Parliamentarian territory.

I dragged myself from under the blankets, for the Diggers were up before daybreak and expected women to be in the kitchen early. When I tugged open the shutters, I gave a cry of surprise. Snow was falling thick and fast, eddying past the window like drifts of feathers. Already a thick quilt had dressed the world in white.

Thank God. Sir Simon would not be able to travel in this weather.

I went to wake Abi. 'Snow,' I mimed, smiling, and fluttering my fingers to imitate the falling flakes.

Abi leapt up out of bed.

'Dress warm,' I said. 'Your chest is still weak.'

Downstairs, the men were clearing the yard, but as quick as they cleared it, more snow fell, until they could see no more than a few feet in front of them, and their shoulders and hats were plastered with white. Cutch was the last to come inside, after valiantly shovelling for all he was worth. But finally even he had to admit defeat.

'It's set in, good and proper,' he said. 'We can't fight nature. Best do work indoors if we can.'

The men sat down around the kitchen table. The room was full of dripping cloaks, muddy boots and the smell of wet cloth. The room seemed suddenly cramped. The fire smoked, seeming to cough for lack of wood. The men began to discuss what might happen if the winter crops could not be sown, and with a great deal of mumbling and grumbling. At length when they showed no sign of removing themselves from the kitchen or finding anything useful to do, Cutch stood up and said he needed help in the stables if anyone would care to join him.

All seemed to think this work better than hanging around the house so they put on their coats and cloaks and followed him out into the blizzard.

'What shall we cook?' Abi asked. 'There's no flour left for bread, and only a handful of barley.'

'We'll just have to be hungry,' Margery said. 'We can go nowhere in this weather.'

'Are there no apples stored in the roof space?' I asked.

'There are a few,' Abi said, 'but I was saving them for the Yule celebrations next week.'

'There'll be no Christmas, if Cromwell has his way,' Margery said. 'We'd best get them apples down, we need to feed the men something.'

'Come on then,' Abi said. 'We'll go and see what's there. Kate, would you fetch some more wood?'

I resisted the urge to refuse. I still could not get used to the idea that someone else could give me orders, and all Diggers must be equal.

The woodpile was reduced to just a small pile of logs. The log basket bruised my hip as I lugged it back, my skirts dragging on the snow. My legs were leaden, the cold seemed to reach inside my bones. I could not understand why I was suddenly so tired. Perhaps grief made me so.

There was not enough wood to feed anything other than the kitchen fire and the house was icy, marooned in a sea of white. Drifts had come as high as the window ledges, and it seemed unlikely anyone could get to the village, even if we had coin to buy food.

The fare that night was an even thinner gruel, with no bread, but we had found the apples and made a mash, which at least was hot and sweet. Some of the children began to grizzle that they were still hungry, but the mothers tried to distract them by playing cat's cradle.

The next week things were worse. We dare not mention Christmas because there was nothing at all in the larder and we were a big company. The men had set out through the drifts to try to snare a winter hare. They could not bear the sound of the children crying for food. Abi and I kept ourselves busy cutting down clothing to make extra layers. Unlike the men, the mending and sewing brought us women together, but then we were in the only warm place in the house. The hard task of hunting in this icy landscape made the men cantankerous.

By nightfall there was still no sign of them, until at last the door burst open and the men brought in a draught of freezing air. Barton flung something down on the table. A skinny hare, and a brace of robins. The robins lay on the table; their necks broken, their eyes dull over their tiny beaks.

'Not much, is it, for a day's hunting,' he said bitterly.

'Better than nothing,' I said.

'We should never have left the village. At least there we could go to a neighbour,' Barton said.

'Your neighbours live here – that's what being a community is about,' I said.

'Seems to me that we men do all the work and you sit by the fire.'

'Now Seth, that's not fair,' Margery said. 'We've been busy all day.'

'Does she do her fair share though, or is this just another way she gets us to be her labour force? Who benefits from this most, eh? We've been fools, all of us. We've come here and done her labour for her with no pay or recompense. It's not right, that.'

I was so angry I could hardly breathe. 'I invited you here from the goodness of my heart—'

'You mean because you saw a way to profit from us.'

'Profit from you? I have done all the same tasks you have, have not shirked a single one. Who salted the beef? Who sewed in the dark to give your children warm petticoats?'

'Old habits die hard. You treat us like we're servants, not equals.'

'That's not true. You can't bear the fact that I treat you like an equal, because I'm a woman, and you're not used to a woman speaking her mind so freely. Yet that's what the Diggers creed tells you it is right to do.'

'How dare you suggest such a thing? I respect women well enough, but not those who lord themselves above us. We came here in good faith, yet our labour's been abused from the very start.'

'Then go. I don't want you here if you're going to be so unmannerly.'

'The Lady of the Manor's showing her true colours and giving us our marching orders, is she? Well we're going anyway. I'm not taking cheek like that from a young flibbertigibbet like you, Lady of the Manor or not.'

Margery had been watching this unfold in silent horror. 'Seth! We're not going, not in this weather. You must be mad.'

'You'll do as I say. Am I your husband or not?'

Margery stammered, and stuttered, unable to speak for a moment before she said, 'I'm not bringing my childer out in that snow, Seth Barton, so you can just think again.'

Barton turned on me, undisguised hostility burning in his eyes, 'Look! Look what you've done, with your talk of women speaking their mind. This is your doing. You breed trouble, it follows you like a hound at heel. You're no better than your kin. The Fanshawes always bring a bad smell with them.'

'Now wait—' Margery stood up to remonstrate with him, but she was too late, he slapped her hand away. Moments later the door slammed behind him and a drift of snow skittered across the flagstone floor.

Margery rushed after him, calling, 'Seth! Wait a minute! Seth!' She threw up her hands, 'He's gone off across the back field. Stupid man.'

I was too shocked to speak for a moment. When I finally found words I whispered, 'Do you think he meant it? That I'm making myself above you?'

'He's a fool. Men and their pride. It gets in the way of everything. He don't like to be beholden, see. And you can't help what you are. But I'll not go after him, not in this weather. I've to think of the little ones. He'll be back soon as supper's ready, if he's got any sense.'

It hurt me to pluck those robins, such tiny birds, and the hare was mostly bone too. But everything went into the pot; we could not afford to waste a scrap. But by that evening there was still no sign of Barton. The men had assumed he was in the house, but when he did not appear at the table, Cutch asked me where he was.

'We had a disagreement,' I said, feeling heat rise to my face, 'and he left.'

'Left? In this?' Whistler was puzzled. The men looked to each other. 'Why? Where was he going?'

'Back to the village,' Margery said. 'He was in one of his moods.'

'When?' asked Susan Whistler.

'About four.'

'But that's hours ago!' Deep wrinkles appeared on Cutch's brow.

'We'd best look for him.' Whistler stood wearily and put on his hat.

'Not now, don't go now, not whilst the food's hot,' Susan said, putting out a hand to restrain him.

'No. It'll taste better when he's at the table,' Whistler said. 'We can't sit and eat whilst we're wondering where he is.' He turned to me. 'What did you say to him?'

'She said nothing,' Margery scowled. 'He was just being awkward, the way he is sometimes.'

'Still, I don't like the idea of him out in this blizzard; the wind's up and it's snowing again. We'd best fetch him in.'

'I vote we eat first,' another man said. 'It's his own damned fault, anyway. I say we let him fend for himself.'

Whistler rubbed his beard. 'Those don't sound like Diggers thoughts, Ben. Where's your charity?'

'Don't you preach at me,' Ben wagged a warning finger. 'I'm not giving up a hot supper for some damned fool who's stupid enough to go out on such a night.'

Whistler ignored him. 'It will get harder to catch up with him, the longer we leave it. I say we go now,' he said.

'Whistler's right,' Cutch agreed. 'The snow might be deeper then.'

'We'd best take a vote. All those who want to look for him—' eight men raised their hands. 'All against?' Four men sullenly stuck their hands in the air, knowing they were outnumbered. Within a few minutes the kitchen was empty again.

'Should we eat?' I asked.

Margery nodded. 'Seth's caused a deal of trouble. I'm sorry.'

'It's not your fault,' Abi said. 'They'll be back soon enough. Let's feed the children, then we'll see what's left.'

But the night grew colder and still the men had not returned. A dark foreboding weighed on me like a stone.

Abi stood at the window and shook her head. 'What shall we do? It's still snowing, and it's that deep. It'd be easy to get lost in this blizzard, it would soon cover any signs.'

I went to join her, so we could talk. I put my hand on her arm, 'We can't do anything, except keep the fire in, and the food hot. Where's Margery?'

'Gone up with the little ones. She and Susan took hot bricks for the beds, and she's seeing to Martha for me. But it's that cold in the rooms upstairs you can see your breath. I expect she'll be back soon. She keeps apologising for Seth, poor soul.'

It was gone midnight when the party returned. 'I can see them,' called Abi. 'I can see Cutch.' We all rushed to the window. The men were moving slowly, plastered with white, stumbling through the snow. They carried something between them.

The door opened.

'Clear the table, Kate.' Something about Cutch's tone made me jump to his bidding.

I scooped up the trenchers and spoons and piled them hastily on the sideboard. An instinct told me to move away from the door.

The noise of the men's return brought Susan and Margery hurrying downstairs, all smiles. But they froze on their faces.

Barton was dead. They had found him lying half buried in snow where he had tripped over a hidden rock. He had crawled only a few yards before succumbing to the cold. Now he was laid out on the kitchen table, his weeping wife squeezing at his hand as if the squeezing might bring him back to life. But his blue lips were silent, his heart still in his grey chest. One foot lay at an odd angle.

'We couldn't find him,' Cutch said. 'His leg's broke. Once he'd fallen, the snow covered him over. Then Ben saw something. Seth's shoulder poking out from a drift. We scraped off the snow, tried to blow heat into him. Rubbed his hands, his chest. But he never moved, though we chafed him and chafed him.'

Margery turned to me, her features screwed tight with anguish. 'It's your doing. He said you were bad luck, but I didn't believe him. He was trying to get away from you. I should have listened to him.'

There was an awkward silence in the room, but nobody denied it. It was as if they were all thinking the same.

'He'll need to go home. To be buried in the church,' Margery said, staring at the white face on the table.

'We can't get there,' Whistler said. 'We'll have to wait for the thaw.'

'Or bury him here, in the chapel grounds,' Abi said.

'No,' Margery said, with sudden venom. 'Not here. I want him buried in a proper churchyard, not in Fanshawe ground.'

'He was a Digger, wasn't he? Surely he didn't hold with all that churchifying,' Cutch said. 'He won't mind where he's laid to rest.'

'Hush your mouth.' Margery pulled back her shoulders and made the sign of the cross. 'Maybe God don't approve of the Diggers. Bible says He sees everything we do. I'm not about to gamble with Seth's immortal soul. A proper church burial, and do it right.'

Of course Seth could not come back to chastise her, whatever she did. But I could no longer recognise the Margery I knew. This woman was blank-eyed with a kind of terror, she kept staring at Seth as if staring at him might make him suddenly sit up again.

But of course he did not and that night we were all awoken by a sudden wailing, 'Seth, come back to me, come back to me,' over and over, as if shouting for him might help her understand where he'd gone.

In the icy chamber I put my pillow over my head, but her

keening voice sent chills of apprehension through me. They'd know it was my fault. I should never have argued with him. He might have stayed at home, if I'd held my tongue.

※

Barton's death seemed to change something in the atmosphere. Though Cutch tried to motivate the men with tasks in the yard, the lack of food made us all listless. My stomach made strange flutterings, but I ignored them. We were down to eating a stew that was more hot water than anything else. The men had spent hours digging through the snow to unearth a single turnip, and we had taken dried peas from a pillow and boiled those too. The children had to come first, for I was damned if I would let the men accuse me of taking food from the mouths of children.

The snow continued unabated and we still could not dig our way to the village. Reluctantly we had to bury Seth Barton in the manor grounds. The snow was hard packed ice now, and digging the plot took a whole day for all the men, chipping away at the frozen ground with picks and spades. When the time came to lay him to rest, we did not linger. The wind blew icy round our ears, and our hands and feet were bloodless and numb.

All the way through our prayers we could hear the anguished neighing of Pepper from his stall. His supply of hay had run out and the horses' corn and bran had long since been used for human consumption. How much longer could we survive without sending someone begging?

'We could kill the horse, it might stop that infernal noise,' Ben Potter said. I gave the man a look that could freeze him solid as the ground, and was grateful Abi was not able to hear him.

Worse, the men now seemed to regard me as their enemy, as if it was my fault this calamity of the bad weather had befallen us. We were cooped up too close. The big house seemed useless when we could not heat it and were all huddled together in one room.

'Seth said no good would come of this. Might as well be living in a barn,' grumbled Whistler.

Abi told me to ignore their hostility, that once we were warm and fed, all would come right. But the tension in the atmosphere was drawn taut, like a bowstring.

8

AN UNEASY ALLIANCE

THE DAY the thaw came I heard it before I got out of bed. Even in the dark I could hear dripping, the slide and whump of snow slipping from the roof, the sharp cries of mallards alighting on the flooded fields.

I saw a messenger on horseback pick his way through the slush and went to greet him. Another letter. Cutch was scraping the yard with a shovel, but I could see him watching me. At the sight of my stricken face he put down the spade and came to lay a hand on my shoulder.

'What's in it? What ails you?'

'Sir Simon's in England. Already. What are we going to do? He won't want the Diggers here.' Fear crawled up my spine at the thought that Sir Simon was already riding the road towards us.

'When will he arrive?' Cutch was ever practical.

'The letter was sent from Dover.'

'Maybe we'll have a few days' grace then, to plan what to do, move people out.'

'I can't do that. I owe them too much, they saved Ralph from the noose. And they trusted me. Things haven't been exactly easy either…'

'Well it's either turn them out, or take your chances and face your stepfather's wrath.'

'I'm not giving up. It was Ralph's dream.'

Cutch picked up the spade again. 'Aye. But Ralph's not here to see it, is he? You have to live by your own ideals, not his.' He took a shovel of snow and heaped it to one side, then pausing, turned to me. 'Are you sure you want to do this? You'll be blamed by both sides, you know that?'

I sighed. 'I can't put these people out. What will Whistler think? I need to prove I'm on their side. Otherwise they'll just see me as tarred with my stepfather's brush.'

'What then?'

'Pray, Cutch. Pray that God sees fit to provide him with an accident before he gets here.'

'Don't say such things. It is blasphemy to even think them.'

As soon as the road cleared, our first visitor was Jacob Mallinson. Abi rushed out to greet him, and they went into the main chamber to talk. As I was going out to the horses she blundered past me, eyes brimming with tears. I tried to stop her, but she wouldn't speak, and just hurried on.

'What's happened to Abi?' I said to him.

'Nothing. Why? What's the matter?'

'She seemed upset. What did you say to her?'

'We were just talking about the highway thieves. People have had things stolen from their barns, and from their dairies. I was asking her if anything had gone missing here, that's all.'

'We had a flitch of beef stolen.'

'Yes, she told me, but she couldn't give me any clues as to who took it.'

'It's good the snow's gone, you'll be able to ride over more often.'

'Well, that's what I was explaining to Abi. Now I'm deputy to my father I'll have less time for visiting. We can't have folks scared to go about their business.'

'Have you set a date for the wedding?'

Jacob dropped his gaze. 'Father says it's not a priority at the moment. There'll be time for that later.'

'Did you tell Abi that?'

'Not in so many words... but you have to understand, things have changed now I'm deputy constable. I have a whole community to look to.'

'And so you're too busy to even call on Abi are you? What's going on, Jacob?'

'Nothing. I'm just busy.' He backed away then and went to collect his horse. I hurried inside to find Abi chopping carrots in the kitchen.

'You all right?'

She didn't answer, but she would not look up.

I took hold of her shoulders to look into her face. 'Don't fret,' I said. 'Jacob's just got a little over-zealous with his new position. He'll go back to being the Jacob we knew soon enough.'

'But he hasn't mentioned anything about our betrothal. Not a thing. Not since Ralph died. And he hasn't tried to... well to kiss me, or anything. Do you think he's having second thoughts?'

I cursed Jacob soundly in my mind. 'I'm sure not. He says he's just busy.'

'He wasn't too busy to call again on my sister.'

The bastard. I should have guessed. 'He's been to see Elizabeth?'

'Jacob says she's helping him with scribing his evidence. Why didn't he ask me? I could have—' She stopped as Cutch poked his head around the door.

'Has he gone?'

Abi rubbed her eyes with the back of her hand, picked up the knife again.

'Yes,' I said.

'What did he want?'

'Just asking if we'd had anything stolen. I told him about the beef.'

Cutch was staring at Abi's red face. He frowned. 'Still after them thieves, is he? Stupid dolt couldn't catch a cold, despite all his galloping about. Don't suppose he's heard anything of your stepfather on his travels?'

'No,' I said. 'But we should have a few more days to think what's best to do.'

※

'They're here!' Abigail burst into my chamber.

Her face was panicked enough to send me to the window, my heart almost leaping from my chest. 'Already. What shall we do?'

Below in the yard the party of men dismounted heavily into the slush, and slung the reins of their horses to the rings in the wall.

'Hoy!' shouted my stepfather, obviously looking for a servant, but naturally nobody appeared. The Diggers were out in the low meadow near the river, sowing winter crops, the women in the kitchen.

I counted my stepfather's men and saw that apart from the corpulent bulk of Sir Simon, I was looking down on the soaked hats and shoulders of three men and a boy.

I heard no warning knock downstairs. Sir Simon simply threw open the front door, and the party clattered in, their swords clanking against the wall.

'What? No welcome?' I heard him exclaim.

'Shall I go down?' Abi looked as scared as I was.

'We'll go together.'

When we entered the parlour, Sir Simon turned, ill humour etched in his frown, 'Well, Katherine, isn't someone going to fetch us ale and a bite to eat? That damn road is full of potholes and boulders, it's taken us all morning from St Albans, and your servants seem a scurvy bunch; not one of them has offered to take our cloaks.' He swivelled his gaze to Abi, whose expression was one of terrified consternation. 'You girl, take our wet cloaks and dry them.'

Abi gathered up the heavy cloaks dripping over a chair, gave a curtsey and like a startled hare, disappeared below.

My stepfather stepped forward, proffered his hand, and I took it, though his flabby face was dour and his eyes held mine with a steely look. *You've not changed*, I thought. His sheer maleness was intimidating. He dropped my hand as if it was a piece of dirt, and moved away.

I glanced at his servants; a youth, probably a messenger boy, and two heavy-set men. 'I'll go and ask Cutch to fetch wood, get a fire lit,' I began. The servant who was staring out of the window turned. My words blocked my throat.

It was Downall, Mallinson's man. Would I never be rid of him? What was he doing here this time? And what business did he have with my stepfather?

He saw my expression and gave me a slight, knowing smile. I folded my arms across my chest. I was rigid, my lack of movement belying the turmoil in my thoughts.

'Your serving maid – have her make up beds for the men,' Sir Simon said, seemingly oblivious to the charge in the air. 'We will be staying only one night, then Downall will be in charge.'

'No.' The word exploded out of me. 'Thomas would forbid it.' I rounded on Downall. 'How dare you. Do you think you can just walk in here and—'

'Enough, Katherine.' My stepfather's voice cut over mine.

'But he broke down our door when—'

'Constable Mallinson recommended him. He says he is familiar with the house.' Sir Simon raised his voice over my objections. 'Besides, the war is done. Over, do you hear? Our differences have been repaired. Bygones are bygones. We need to think to the future.'

As simple as that? It could not be so. Downall's clenching and unclenching fists told me he was as uncomfortable as I was. His eyes fixed mine in a warning. He was well aware that I could tell Sir Simon about the riot last summer. But then, he could tell Sir Simon of my intimacy with Ralph.

We glared at each other with unspoken hostility.

Best to keep quiet. Sir Simon would show me no mercy if he thought I'd been unfaithful to Thomas. But Downall despised the Diggers. What would happen if Downall were put in charge? I needed to think.

'I'll go and call for refreshment and see about airing your chamber, sir,' I said, and fled from the room. On the way to the kitchen I took in great gulps of air. I felt as if my stays were suffocating me. The thought of Downall being in my house was unbearable. I could still see him in my mind's eye, slinging the noose around Ralph's neck.

Abi heard my steps from above and ran out to meet me, her face pale and drawn. 'I saw. Your stepfather's hired Downall. What shall we do?' she whispered.

'Worse – Sir Simon's only staying one day, then we'll be at Downall's mercy. He's wormed his way into my stepfather's favour. God knows how, but he has.'

'But what about—' Abi was protesting but there was no time for argument.

'Sir Simon won't know they're Diggers. He'll just think they're hired hands. Ask the womenfolk to make up beds in the servant's quarters in the west wing,' I said, making my speech as plain as I could. 'Try to keep Sir Simon and his servants in the east wing. East wing, do you understand?'

'I don't see how I can. The menfolk don't like being told what to do.'

'Explain it's only for one night. I'll face up to Sir Simon about Downall; suggest he appoints someone else.'

'But who?'

'Whistler? One of ours anyway.' My head buzzed with trying to keep all my thoughts ordered. 'And if we can placate our people for just one night, we might have a chance of keeping them on. They must act like our servants, invisible, don't create any fuss.'

'You don't know what you're asking. They don't want to be servants, do they? Ralph was always saying that they wanted charge of their own—'

'Have you a better idea?' I snapped.

Abi was silent.

'Then do as I ask.'

When I got back to the parlour with the last watered dregs of our ale, the serving boy had lit a fire with the few sticks in the basket. It smoked and sputtered, for the wood was damp. Downall was at the table, looking over plans of the estate, and Sir Simon was warming his backside against the meagre heat.

Sir Simon nodded at the tray in my hands. 'You're too lax with the servants,' he said. 'Your girl should have brought that up. Still don't know why you keep her on, a deaf girl like that.'

'Can I speak with you alone, sir?'

'Have you heard from my nephew yet?' Sir Simon ignored my request.

'No sir. You can ask *him* why.' I gestured to Downall.

Downall studiously ignored me, his eyes never leaving the papers, but his tensed neck showed he was listening.

'It's not like Thomas,' Sir Simon said. 'He should have arrived with me weeks ago. Have you heard no word at all of his whereabouts?'

'None, sir,' I said.

'Did you not think it strange? Why did you not write to tell me?'

'I assumed Thomas had gone to you, so I saw no cause for worry.'

Sir Simon fixed me with cold eyes. 'A dutiful wife would expect letters from her husband, would she not?'

I flinched. 'Thomas was never in the habit of writing to me. Has he not written to you?'

'No.' Sir Simon was not pleased at me pushing the vexed question back at him. He paced the room. Downall's stillness showed he was listening to all this unfold, like a hawk watching prey.

My question had disturbed my stepfather. He seemed to search for an answer. 'Well it could be that he is still lying low, awaiting better weather and a passage to France.'

'I'm sure you're right,' Downall said, turning to face us. 'He'll be hiding in a safe house somewhere. That is, unless he's been arrested. Cromwell's determined to stamp out the last of the king's sympathisers. Those who have yet to see sense.' It was a veiled threat, and from my stepfather's face I could see he knew it.

Sir Simon pursed his lips, obviously holding back a retort. It took him effort to do so. Six months ago he would have drawn his sword on Downall for such a statement. Instead, he said, 'Constable Mallinson suggests I should make enquiries with the stage coach companies for news of my nephew.' He flicked his eyes meaningfully to Downall. 'Mallinson, at least, seems to be a reasonable man. Perhaps he's right, and they can tell us something about where Thomas went.'

'Can I talk to you alone, sir?' I asked again.

He scrutinised my face. 'Is it about my nephew?'

'Yes,' I lied.

'Very well. Downall, arrange for a servant to take my bags upstairs.' Downall stood from the plans, and bowed, but it looked as though it hurt him to do so. 'And you, Venner,' my stepfather waved at his other servant, 'go and dry the tack and see to the horses.'

Moments later, I was alone with Sir Simon and the boy. I felt like I was twelve years old again. I still remembered the sound of my stepfather's whip as it cut through the air, and the sudden stinging pain. The old fear rose up, but I stiffened my spine, refusing to let him cow me.

'Well?' my stepfather asked.

'Downall's not to be trusted. Shortly after the king fled into exile, he roused up the other men in the village to try and take over this house with his Puritan rabble. They came in the night, armed with picks and shovels.'

'What about Thomas? Did he—?'

'Thomas and another Royalist, Copthorne, tried to defend the house against them, but it was hopeless. Downall's men were like a pack of dogs, wild with anger. And there were too many. They tore through the house and...' I pushed away my emotions, took a deep breath. I tried to make my account of it factual; gave him the bare bones of it, 'Downall would have killed Thomas if he hadn't fled. His men would have torn him limb from limb.'

'You think I don't know all this? You're wrong.' Sir Simon's face twisted in a half-smile. He lowered his voice. 'I know precisely what Downall is. A mealy-mouthed God-botherer and a traitor to the king. But we have had to come to an agreement now. I need him. He has friends in the new Protectorate. Constable Mallinson is using him to ensure we uphold the new regime. I had no choice but to employ him.'

I looked away. It was not what I wanted to hear.

My stepfather continued, 'They trust him – more fools, they. He's somehow wrangled himself onto the sequestration committee for this area. We have a good chance of keeping this house only if we show penance and loyalty to Cromwell's rump of a Parliament. And common men like Downall.' He spat out the words with derision.

'What then? What will happen to this house?'

'If they don't take it from us, we'll sell. We need the coin if Thomas is to make his way in France. England's finished. God knows, I can't live with Cromwell's law. And life's costly at the French court. You'll find that out for yourself soon enough.'

I was silent. I was not going to France. I knew that with certainty, but it was wisest to say nothing. Instead I asked, 'Has Thomas no savings?'

'The King's Army ruined us,' my stepfather said bitterly, slumping into a chair. 'It ate up all our reserves. And all for what? The young king's not like his father, he cares not a damn farthing for any of us. As soon as we find Thomas, I shall arrange your passage to the French court. The war has interrupted your lives for far too long, it is time to think about an heir, someone to carry on the Fanshawe name.'

No. The idea of surrendering my body to Thomas Fanshawe was unthinkable. There would never be a son to carry on the Fanshawe name, I thought. A rush of grief for Ralph blinded my eyes with tears. I turned away.

When I looked back, it was to see Sir Simon leaning on the mantel to warm his knees. 'Constable Mallinson knows a family from London who wish to view the estate and they might make us a decent offer. Damned Puritans, no doubt. But it will be good to be rid of the Ferrers' lands, they've been nothing but an encumbrance.'

'The deeds are in Thomas's name. You cannot sell unless Thomas agrees and he's—'

'He'll sell, Katherine.' My stepfather's expression told me that when he found him, he would bully Thomas into acceptance as he usually did. It wouldn't surprise me if Thomas had gone missing on purpose, simply to avoid his overbearing uncle. 'And in the meantime, you need not see Downall. He is lodging in the village. He will come daily to oversee the estate. It's no business for a girl like you. You will keep out of his way and leave the business to him. He has his orders and will answer to me, and to Mallinson.' Sir Simon sat down heavily, and stretched his feet towards the fire.

I thought of Whistler and the others. 'Can't we have someone else?' I took a deep breath, 'Some of the villagers are living in to help with the land. There's a man called Whistler and he—' I paused. A noise outside the door.

'And how are you paying them, these villagers?' Sir Simon asked.

'They're working for nothing, for a share in the produce...' I tailed off. Downall appeared in the doorway, smirking.

Sir Simon stared up at me. 'For nothing, you say?' He laughed. 'Maybe you're turning into a Fanshawe after all.'

Downall's presence stifled any reply. Something warned me, he'd heard every word I said.

Sir Simon dismissed me. Thank the Lord, he and Downall spent the afternoon in the old library, whilst Sir Simon told him how to run the estate. During this time, I chivvied Abi and Cutch to move everyone's possessions into the west wing.

Of course that evening, when the Diggers found out they'd been moved, there was grumbling.

'They're not happy, Kate,' Abi said, as we brought back plates from the west wing. 'They know something's not right, and it's stirring up ill feeling. Whistler saw Downall as he left to go home. There's never been love lost between them. And now you've moved them to smaller quarters they're calling you tight-fisted, that you're squeezing them for their labour.'

'It's just one night,' I said. 'One night, then Sir Simon will be gone.'

'What about Downall?' Abi said.

'I don't know. You could try talking to Jacob, see if he can get his father to send someone else.'

'If I ever see him,' she said. She swallowed, looked away. 'The lack of a dowry has changed things between us.'

I saw the hurt in her eyes. 'He still cares, Abi, I'm sure of it,' I said.

'Then why doesn't he come? Do you think he's found someone else?'

'Nonsense,' I said briskly. 'Stop these foolish thoughts and help me dry.' I turned away; scrubbed hard at the platters in the sink.

9

THE BROKEN PROMISE

THE NEXT MORNING I had to eat with my stepfather. The way he chewed his cold meat and spat out the gristle made my stomach heave. I picked at the crust of my bread, anxious that he should get to horse and be on his way, but our breakfast was interrupted by a loud hammering at the door.

'Answer it, boy,' Sir Simon said.

A few moments later the boy stood to one side to allow Constable Mallinson and Downall to come in.

Sir Simon wiped his mouth with a napkin, and stood.

'Fanshawe,' Mallinson extended his hand. 'I'm glad you are here at last. You have saved me issuing warrants for non-attendance at church. Downall tells me you are willing to put your allegiance to Parliament, so I'm assuming you will sort out the troublemakers who are lodging on your nephew's land.'

Downall shot me a triumphant look. I stiffened, heart sinking, fearing what was to come.

Sir Simon remained standing, looking to me for an explanation, his expression grim. I felt a cold sweat break on my forehead, but could not think of what to say. So I lowered my gaze, said nothing, waiting for the axe to fall.

'What troublemakers are these?' Sir Simon asked.

'Downall alerted me,' Mallinson said. 'He's been keeping a close watch on who came and went here. He came across Mr Soper in a tavern, and he said his cousin Margery Barton's being used by the Fanshawes as slave labour. He asked him what he meant, and with a little persuasion he confirmed what Downall had suspected.'

No persuasion, I thought. Ned Soper's mouth was legendary.

'And what's that?' Sir Simon was impatient, picking at his teeth with a toothpick.

'He says you're housing irregular meetings here, meetings of Winstanley's men, the Diggers. None of the people working here have been seen at church for the past months, and that's an offence.'

'Katherine?' Sir Simon turned his eyes to me, and I could feel the threat in them.

'We couldn't get to church because of the weather,' I said. 'The snow.'

'Do you deny you're housing dissenters?' asked Mallinson.

I sighed. 'Yes, there are men working here, and yes, they believe in Winstanley's ways. The Diggers' ways. But their beliefs are no business of mine. They're my workers, that's all.'

'The law is clear against meetings and conventicles,' Downall said. 'Cromwell won't permit any gathering against the true church.'

'It's not about the church,' I burst out. 'It's about not wasting good land. What choice did I have, Constable Mallinson, answer me that? So many dead in the wars, it doesn't pay to be too particular.'

'Wait! You employ these dissenters without my knowledge?' Sir Simon stepped towards me.

'Not employ, sir, no,' I said bitterly. 'Thomas is missing, and you've sent me nothing. How was I supposed to survive? On fresh air? I've no coin to employ people. The men and women working here work from the good of their hearts. For a share in the produce, and a roof over their heads. What can be ill with that?'

'Enough.' Sir Simon strode over as if to strike me, but then he let his hand fall. 'I will talk with you on this matter later, Katherine. Leave us.'

I braced my shoulders. 'I will not. I have run this household for months without—'

'Leave us!' Sir Simon's voice dropped to a growl.

His servant, Venner, approached to take hold of me. 'Don't you dare to touch me! I'll be in the small parlour,' I said icily, 'if I'm to be thrown from my own withdrawing room.'

But I did not go into the small parlour. Instead I hovered beyond the door, listening to the low rumble of voices beyond. I cursed the solid oak thickness of our doors that would not let me hear the conversation. I picked up only fragments; Thomas's name, my own name. My stepfather's slightly nasal voice could be heard with an unusually grovelling tone.

The ring of the servant's bell below startled me into movement.

As I went down towards the kitchen I almost bumped into Abi coming up. 'I saw the kerchief flutter,' she said. Abi had a white rag tied to the bell hammer to alert her to its ring. 'What is it?'

'I don't know. They threw me from the room. Mallinson and Downall are here, and they probably want refreshment. But they know about the Diggers living here. I don't know what to—'

The door swung open in a great draught. Sir Simon's corpulent bulk filled the space. He ignored me and addressed Abi. 'Girl. Fetch everyone who works on the estate and have them line up on the drive.'

Abi looked to me for confirmation, but I could do nothing but shake my head. He was the master of the house in Thomas's absence, and besides, one look at his bull-like face told me it was hopeless to refuse.

Sir Simon raised a hand towards Abi. 'What are you waiting for? Now!'

Abi scuttled away.

I hoped the men and women wouldn't agree to come, but they were all there, standing in a knot, close together in the drizzle, like sheep huddled in a field. Even Margery and Susan, who had their arms around their children's shoulders as if to protect them. Their faces were apprehensive. They knew trouble was coming.

'You won't make them go, will you?' I pleaded, with Sir Simon, fearing the worst. 'They've given us more than two months of hard work.'

But Sir Simon ignored me, stepped out onto the front steps, his fingers stuck in his waistcoat to display his barrel-like chest, Downall and Venner flanking his sides.

'Sir, I beg you…'

'Be quiet,' he snapped.

Before us the crowd were silent, waiting.

Sir Simon screwed up his mouth as if to gather his words before spitting out, 'Circumstances have changed. We no longer have need of your services.' An indignant muttering amongst the men. 'I expect you to have removed your personal belongings and to be off this land by dusk. Any goods left behind will be burnt—'

'Now just wait a minute—' The men began to protest.

'—and any person left behind will be arrested,' Sir Simon shouted over them. 'Do I make myself clear?'

'What about wages or compensation?' Potter said, stepping

forward. 'We worked hard to plant and sow this land and have had no harvest yet. My wife filled your belly last night and we're not leaving until I have—'

'Lady Katherine tells me you worked for shelter and a roof over your head. So you have already been recompensed. We owe you nothing.'

'That's not what I said!' I took hold of my stepfather's arm, but he whipped his arm away with an impatient gesture.

'Don't go!' I shouted to Whistler, but Sir Simon's hand caught me on the side of the cheek with a stinging slap that made me wince.

'You stupid girl,' he said, through clenched teeth. 'Don't you see what you've done? I had to grovel to gain us ground in Cromwell's favour and you do this! Undo all my work behind my back.'

'Sir, be reasonable,' I said. 'They have small children. It's raining. We can't just—'

'Get back inside. I won't take interference from you.' Sir Simon pushed me through the front door and slammed it in my face. When I tried to open it I found someone was holding the handle from the other side. I twisted the handle with all my might but it would not budge.

I ran to the window, but the Diggers were already dispersing. Why? Why weren't they fighting back? But fighting had never been their way, and the threat of arrest had unmanned them. It made me want to weep, that they should give up so easily. That a man like my stepfather should find it so easy to bully them. I watched Whistler deliberately spit on our front step.

Below, the repeated bang of the kitchen door. I ran pell-mell down the stairs.

Margery was in the kitchen throwing a few remaining vegetables into a sack. At my arrival she pulled her apron off the hook.

'Margery, wait—'

She shoved me away. 'Don't you try your oily words with me! We trusted you. Now look what a mess we're in. Winter, and no roof over our heads and nowhere to go. Seth was right. You're like all the rest. Don't give a fig for anyone but yourself.'

'That's not true! It's not my fault that—'

'No. Nothing's ever your fault is it? My Seth would still be alive if it wasn't for you. Bitch. Now get out of my way.' She hustled by me and up the stairs.

A few moments later she marched down. She passed without a word, the bundle of her bedding thrust under her arm, a cloth bag full of clothing slung over her back. She was dragging her youngest boy by the wrist. He was crying, but she yanked him out of the kitchen door.

A clatter of boots on the stairs and Abi's little sister, Martha, appeared. 'Jonty,' she cried. 'Wait for me!'

'No,' I said catching her around the waist, 'you can't go with them.'

'Why? I want to play with Jonty.' She struggled and kicked until a crack on the shin forced me to let go. I followed her to the open door. The Diggers were hurrying down the drive, arms full of their possessions, the men shouldering spades and hoes. They strode away with their heads down, as though they could not get away quick enough, the children tagging behind, hauled away by impatient parents.

'Jonty!' Martha cried again, running after her friend. 'Wait for me!'

Jonty turned to look, but Margery slapped him, and thrust him forwards. She yelled at Martha, 'Get on home. We don't want you.'

Martha's face crumpled. She stood disconsolate on the driveway, fingers pulling on the corner of her apron.

I ran to comfort her, but she screamed, 'Go away!' at me and ran to the stables. None of the Diggers looked back.

The sight of their backs filled me with sudden weariness. The dream was over. I'd failed. I sat down at the kitchen table, and pressed my arm against my forehead. 'I'm sorry, Ralph,' I whispered.

Abi came in through the back door, her face white, Martha gathered up onto her hip like a much younger child. 'Hush now, baby,' she said. 'Run upstairs and wash your face, then I'll play chickens with you.'

Martha trailed upstairs, heavy-footed.

Abi turned to me, 'They've gone. What shall we do?'

'Don't you want to join them?' The words were bitter.

'Don't be daft. Your stepfather told me I could stay. I'll warrant he fears he'll lose his dinner without a servant in the kitchen. But I can't keep Martha here; he won't have it.'

'You could go.'

'Where to? To Elizabeth? She wouldn't thank me. And I couldn't bear to go to mother's cottage,' she paused, twisting her mouth. 'Too many bad memories. And I don't want to leave you here alone with Downall. No. I'll take Martha back to the vicarage. She had company there. You and I will see this out together.'

'I thought to make the Diggers my friends, but they always saw me as something different. Now they'll hate me.' I slumped back into the chair.

'It's not your fault,' Abi said.

'Ralph would be disappointed in me. I've let him down.'

'He'll know you tried.'

'Trying's not enough! All that work, and they got not a penny for it. No wonder they hate me.'

'They'll get over it in time, Kate. It's not in their natures to bear grudges for long.'

'But it's not fair. I'll pay them for their work somehow, if it's the last thing I do. I'll make them see that I'm on their side.' I was almost talking to myself.

'How? You have no money. Thomas is still missing. Where will you get coin to pay them with?'

New resolve fired through my veins. 'I don't know, but I'll do it. I'll prove to them that I'm not like my stepfather – that I'm a Digger at heart.'

10

HOUSE BUYERS

THE NEXT DAY Sir Simon left to look for Thomas in London, and sort out some of his trading affairs. Downall soon replaced the Diggers with dark-dressed men of his own choosing, who saw him as cock of the roost. I overheard one of them saying his brother wouldn't work for us because the Fanshawes were bad luck and made you work for nothing.

I knew where that rumour had come from and it hurt. I was still determined to make it up to the Diggers somehow. I couldn't bear it that Ralph's friends thought ill of me.

A week later, Sir Simon sent his servant Venner back to us. With him came a party of well-dressed men from the city; Gawthorpe, a fat merchant tailor, and his two hefty sons. The Gawthorpes were newly wealthy, judging by their fine leather boots and velvet doublets, but rough. They wore heavy white Puritan collars that needed a good wash.

My mother would have thought them common and coarse, but that was how things were now the wars were over. Aristocratic blood had fled abroad. I did not like the look of them, but then I would not like the look of anyone who wanted to cast me out of my own home, for these were the men who wanted to buy the manor.

And Sir Simon had deliberately neglected to inform me they were coming.

I was icy with them, but the father ignored me as Venner took them round the rooms. The sons stared at me morosely, as if I was an unwelcome servant.

I assured them that all the rooms were draughty, but Gawthorpe took no notice and made encouraging comments about the possible renovation of the dining hall, the parlour and the library. Venner had obviously briefed them about my position beforehand and waxed forth about what a bargain the estate was.

Venner took them into the study to feed them madeira wine, and presumably secure an offer for the house.

The sons asked about the hunting.

'Finest deer park in Hertfordshire,' Venner said. 'There's two hundred head in those woods.'

A lie. Our deer had been taken by the Roundheads in the wars. Sickened, I went out to the stables to feed Blaze some extra oats, and to talk to Cutch.

'They'll buy,' I said gloomily.

'What will you do then?' Cutch shut the stable door on the visitors' horses and flopped down on a heap of hay.

'My stepfather expects me to go to France. He won't admit Thomas might be dead. Obviously I don't want to go.'

'Have you any savings?'

'None. The wars took everything I had. And if I disobey, and refuse to go to France my stepfather has the power to imprison me, or get me transported.'

'He doesn't know about Ralph though, does he?'

Our conversation was interrupted by voices in the yard. We pulled the door closed and listened. I pressed my ear to the crack in the door.

'So you're saying the tenants are trouble?' The rough-edged voice of Gawthorpe.

'They're an unruly, unlettered lot,' I heard Downall say. 'Hard to manage. Makes it difficult to turn a profit.'

Cutch and I looked to each other in amazement.

'But the deer park – Venner told me it was the biggest in Hertfordshire.'

'Was,' Downall said. 'Before the wars. It's just a few head of deer now. I think you'll find all the fences are in need of repair, and the villagers – well, they're not averse to a spot of poaching.'

'So you're saying it's not a good buy?'

'Wouldn't touch it with a horsewhip, myself,' Downall said. 'Roof leaks too.'

'Oh Lord. Sounds bad, father,' came a younger voice.

'But we'd brought coin as a deposit!' I heard the splutter in Gawthorpe's voice. 'We'd hoped to seal the transaction. Fanshawe told us to talk to the sequestration committee and they would assist with the paperwork. We've set aside a week.'

'Well, it's up to you, but...' Downall let his words hang.

'Damn it,' Gawthorpe said. 'We'd thought it a bargain, but it seems we were duped. My thanks, sir, you have saved us a lot of heartache. We owe you a favour.'

'Not at all, not at all.' Downall's voice was more than usually ingratiating.

Cutch raised his eyebrows at me. It was obvious Downall did not want them to buy. But why?

We had no time to ponder it, as their footsteps announced the Gawthorpes' arrival to collect the horses and carriage. Cutch leapt up to go and turn the horses. I peeped out of the door to see Gawthorpe shake hands with Downall. The two hefty sons clambered into the carriage. Through the open door I saw their big black-bound trunk. I imagined its weight, the sift of coin through my fingers.

'Sir Simon would spit feathers if he knew Downall had lost him the sale,' Cutch said, when they'd gone.

'Is Downall just intent on making trouble, or is there another reason? I don't trust him.'

Cutch sighed. 'Sooner or later the house will sell. You have to face it.'

But I was not thinking of that. I was still thinking of the Gawthorpes' money chest. The thought of the Gawthorpe's coin had stuck in my mind like a burr sticking to worsted. If I had that trunk, there would be plenty there to pay the Diggers for their work. And the Gawthorpes were rich; they had plenty.

That night when everyone was asleep, I saddled Blaze and rode out through the village. The Gawthorpes would be at The Crown. There was nowhere else to stay. I rode round the back lane to see that their carriage was still parked there. That trunk full of coin would be upstairs with them now, whilst they snored. I imagined opening it, plunging my wrists into the rattle of gold.

For a long time I stared up at the inn, ruminating. The moon was a fine sliver, a perfect night for highway thieves. I thought of those other highwaymen, of poor Mrs Binch's face. Why should those men be the only thieves on the road? There was no sign of them now. Despite his enthusiasm, Jacob Mallinson had not been able to apprehend them. Common sense told me they were probably in another county by now.

The thought rooted and would not let go. I had turned highway thief once before, and I could do it again.

All it needed was courage.

I thought of Ralph, of how much he'd sacrificed for his ideals. I could suffocate under Sir Simon's ways, or I could take fate into my own hands. Reckless, I pulled on the reins to turn, and with a yell, set my heels to my horse's flanks.

Later, in my chamber, I took out a quill and began to write a list of the Diggers who had worked my land. I was so feverish with excitement that my hand shook. I could not sleep. Now the idea had come to me, I was impatient to put it into action. I'd need to find out where the Diggers lodged, and a way of leaving each of them a bag of money where it could be easily found.

Above all, it felt good to be going against my stepfather's orders. Since I was twelve years old I had been bartered and bought. But no more. I would make my choice. The Fanshawes thought I needed them, but I needed no one. Ralph was right. Before, my wealth had been a curse, but I'd make this wealth a blessing. The prospect made a frisson of fear trickle up my back.

The next morning I was up at dawn. My stepfather had left a pair of antiquated flintlocks in the desk drawer of the study. I had seen them when I went for writing paper and quill. After that, I went to the lumber room where they kept hunting weapons. There I took some fish-gutting knives for cutting open purses, flinching at the sight of their sharp edges.

I took a sack and filled it with practical clothes. I had not many, but I took a pair of Whistler's rough-weave breeches that had been left behind, and Thomas's boots from his room. A dark felt hat of my own would hide my hair. I cursed the fact it was so thick and unruly. With my own black wool mourning cloak over my clothes, I would pass for a man.

I imagined Whistler finding a bag of coin and wondering where it had come from, his broad face creasing up in puzzlement. And then I imagined him finding out later who had left it, and his admiration and distress that he'd doubted me. I would be a secret benefactor, and make Ralph proud of me. I wished he could see me; I ached for him still.

The Diggers would change their minds about me. When they saw how I had put my life on the line for them, they'd realise I was one of them after all.

11

AN UNWANTED PROPOSAL

Downall arrived for work the next day and took the servants into the study to give them the day's instructions. It was like when Grice used to be overseer. I was shut out of all the management of my own house. I took matters into my own hands and listened outside the door. I needed to know where everyone would be that evening.

Yesterday Cutch had been to the farrier in the village. He told me the Gawthorpes had been there just before him with their horses, because they were to leave after supper tonight. Once I heard Downall dismiss the servants, I hurried away and I was halfway down the stairs when Venner called after me, 'Master wants to see you.'

'Master?' I filled my voice with as much sarcasm as I could.

'Mr Downall. He wants you to go in.'

'I'm busy.' I started to walk away.

Downall opened the door, and seeing me there, called me in. I stood reluctantly before the desk, whilst he sat, lounging, a pile of paperwork before him.

'Where do you go to?' He asked. 'The servants say you rode out last night and were gone many hours.'

'Just riding,' I said. 'I like to be out in the air.'

'At night? Perhaps I could accompany you, then, on one of your evening rides.'

My heart was beating fast in my bodice. 'I prefer to go alone.' I turned to go. I did not want this conversation with him. And I felt panic rising. I had a sudden vision of being followed. I must be careful.

Downall came round from the desk to tower over me. 'Do you know where Thomas Fanshawe is?' His question took me by surprise, and it must have showed. 'You do, don't you?'

'No,' I said. 'All I know is that he ran away. When you broke down our door and Copthorne came and tried to hold us all hostage. I don't know where my husband is now.'

'So he could be dead, for all you know?'

I looked him in the eye. 'He could be anywhere. There are so many missing since the wars. Excuse me.' I tried to step past him but Downall delayed me with an outstretched arm.

'Best to let the past go,' he said, lifting my chin with one finger, 'as I have. If your husband is dead, you will be free to marry.'

'It is too early to think of that.' I backed away.

'Once we know Thomas's fate, I will be pursuing my suit with your stepfather. He will see the political advantages a match between us will bring.'

I cringed. The thought filled me with revulsion. Downall was an old man. 'I could never marry you.'

'Never? I don't think you will have a choice if it is what Sir Simon commands. And he will command it, I'll see to that. If Thomas is dead, the lands pass to Sir Simon as the nearest male heir. You would be a burden on your stepfather with no husband. He will own your land and all your wealth. You will be nothing unless you marry. It will be me, or some other of your stepfather's choosing. But if you wed me, you can stay here, in your family home.'

'No.' I thought of Ralph and knew I had to get out of the room before I said something disastrous. 'I will speak to my stepfather on this matter. Now let me pass.'

He stood aside, his manner casual, though his voice had an edge. 'Do that. Sir Simon will think my way, or I will see to it that the sequestration committee take his lands.'

12
HIGHWAYWOMAN

I KEPT out of Downall's sight until he left at sunset for his lodgings. I watched his thick neck above his Puritan collar as he trotted away, and breathed a sigh of relief. The night was dark, but I waited until gone seven. I fastened a heavy taffeta skirt over my men's clothes in case I was seen by the servants. The waistband was uncomfortably tight, and I was a few moments trying to get the strings to meet over the bulk of Whistler's tweed breeches.

Above me, the voice of Venner as he gave Abi instructions, and outside, the mournful hoot of an owl. I tiptoed down the stairs, creaked open the side door, then hurried across the yard into the stalls. No sign of Cutch. Probably in the tack room cleaning the saddlery, or mending harness. I was glad, because he might have tried to stop me. I pulled off my heavy taffeta skirt and stuffed it down into an empty barrel. Then I jammed the velveteen hat tight over my hair and tied the cords under my chin. A kerchief completed my disguise.

I bridled Blaze and he whickered at me as I tiptoed to collect the saddle. In the dark I had to do everything by feel. I tied two sacks either side of the pommel for my spoils. A wave of tiredness washed over me. I hesitated. Had I lost leave of my senses?

I turned to look at the house. It wasn't too late to stop this madness. I could turn back, go inside, out of danger, back to the light. Pretend I had never thought of the idea. I held my arms against my belly, hugging myself, uncertain.

From here the domed towers of the manor were just visible against the even blacker sky. Otherwise the house was just like a splash of ink against black silk. My house. My inheritance. A sharp twinge of regret, a longing, made tears prickle at my lashes. I was homesick, I realised. Not for that – not for Markyate Manor, but for a home I had never really possessed. For all the homes that I had imagined as a child; the farmsteads where a mother laid out the butter and eggs for breakfast, the town houses in winter where visitors were led to a hot fire and given a posset in an ale cup to warm their hands.

But though I had willed it otherwise, Markyate Manor had been none of these. My stepfather had kept his whip over the fireplace as a reminder of his authority. And he had used it. The Diggers had been the only folk who offered me a welcome, and now that was ruined.

I could still make amends - give them recompense, if I had courage.

'You can do it,' Ralph's voice echoed in my head.

I turned sharply, stuck a foot in the stirrup and leapt astride. Spooked by this night-time adventure, Blaze shot into a gallop.

I did not know then that someone was on the drive watching me go. And when I rounded the bend, I did not see the other horse until I heard the hoof beats behind me.

At first I thought it was Blaze's hooves, but as the sound doubled, I glanced over my shoulder. The glint of a bit, a white star on the horse's head, a white sock on the foreleg. One horse, one rider. Cloaked, no hat. Broad shoulders. A man. What did he want?

I daren't slow down. It couldn't be anything good, I knew that much. I pushed on. He was gaining on me, but I applied my heels and Blaze sped on. Thoughts of the highway thieves, the feeling of the muzzle of the gun, flashed through my mind. I could hear nothing now except the sound of my own breath, thick in my throat, over the pounding of Blaze's hooves.

I veered left into the bridleway, branches whipped past my face. I ventured another quick look back. He was right behind me, his horse's mouth white with foam. But I knew the set of that jaw, the bristle of sandy hair. Downall. I kicked Blaze on, but the track twisted like a noose and we were forced to slow. Moments later I felt his thigh bang into mine as he came alongside and reached to grab the rein with his hand. I lashed out at him with the slack of my reins.

'Stop!' he shouted, making a fresh attempt to grab Blaze by the bridle. 'Where are you going?'

I did not answer. I was trying to manoeuvre Blaze past him, but Blaze was blocked in by the bigger horse. As he leaned to grab the bridle, I threw another lash at him with all my strength. The end of the reins caught him full in the face. He cursed and let go.

In the distance, a shot, then another. A third, and Blaze half reared.

Somewhere to the left of us. The noise ricocheted. Downall turned to look.

It was enough. I kicked Blaze on and he shot down the path. A branch scraped at my face and caught in my hair, tearing at the roots. My eyes watered so much I could not see, but I did not dare stop even to look back.

I crouched flat to Blaze's neck, clinging to his mane, and veered left and right into the forest, not knowing where I was going, just choosing the smallest tracks where a bigger horse and rider would struggle to follow. My chest thumped uncomfortably, I gasped for breath. We came to a dense scrub of brush and holly and I forced Blaze through it. Only on the other side did I pause to listen. Blaze was panting, his flanks heaving against my shaking legs. I listened, but heard no other hoof beats.

I slumped forward in the saddle, my blood fizzing in my veins. Downall knew now that I was dressed as a man. But I had done nothing. He could prove nothing.

But though I waited a half hour or more, there was no other noise from the forest except the soft patter of a drizzle that had just begun to fall. My eyes had become accustomed to the dark, and now I could pick out the shapes of the trees and the silvery trail of the track, where the earth was pale and bare.

I had no idea where I was, I realised. Which way?

I patted Blaze's neck, to reassure him. Perhaps he would know the way. Not back the way I had come. I could not risk meeting Downall again on the track. I let the reins hang loose, let Blaze pick his way through the trees. As we went, I put my hand to my cheek, and my fingers caught on a dried crust of blood.

Blaze was surefooted and certain. I hoped he'd find his way to the main road, and sure enough, the wider dirt road lay just beyond the trees. I looked both ways but all was quiet. I rode slowly, on the verge next to the road to muffle my hooves. Perhaps I had missed the Gawthorpes. Those shots did not bode well, and worse, Downall was still out there somewhere. I was nauseous, uncertain whether to go or stay.

I turned for home. I'd gone a mere half mile when a coach and horses loomed out of the darkness towards me. Wary, I withdrew into the shelter of the trees, but the horses trotted erratically, the carriage yawing from one side of the road to the other.

There was no driver. At the sight of another horse on the road, the horses slowed the carriage to a halt.

It was eerie, this driverless carriage. I waited.

Nobody leaned out to see what the problem was. I slid out the pistol from the pack on Blaze's withers, then dismounted and hitched my reins to a tree. The carriage was still, but as I got nearer I saw the door was hanging open, as if no one had bothered to shut it. The insignia on the side was familiar. The eagle and claw of the Gawthorpes' carriage.

I approached from the front and steadied the horses. They jittered and trembled in their traces. Inch by inch I crept towards the carriage door. A stockinged foot was jamming it open. A foot with no shoe.

Nearer. In one quick movement I flung it wide.

Inside lay the crumpled figure of one of the Gawthorpe boys. A shot wound dribbled like a black blot on his temple. I rocked him, called him, but he was lifeless. The rest of the carriage was empty. There was no sign of his father or his brother.

Hastily, I stepped away. Looked over my shoulder. I was too late. I had to get out of here. Some other thief had stolen the trunk of gold, the one that should have been mine, and the thief could be still in the woods somewhere. I rode tentatively along the verge, eyes skinning the landscape.

Two lumps of dark in the road. I stayed in the saddle, ready to gallop.

The father and the other son. Both dead.

As far as I could tell, both had pistol wounds to the chest. In the ditch at the side of the track, something caught my eye. It was the box, the one they'd brought with them; the deposit for the house.

Was it worth the risk? Hurriedly I dismounted.

Only a few paltry coins remained, as if the highway thieves had been surprised and had been in too much of a hurry to take it all. I stared at the dull shine of the silver discs a moment before scraping them up and pocketing them.

Later that night I rode by Whistler's house. It was an unkempt single-roomed dwelling of brick and lath, with holes in the roof. Outside the door was an upturned milk churn. I righted it,

dropped the coins inside and heard their metallic chink as they landed. After them I pushed a note:
No labour should go unrewarded.

13
MOONLIGHT AND MURDER

THE NEXT DAY I slept longer. My limbs were heavy, and it was past cock crow when I woke. My body was objecting to my new profession, but I didn't want to listen to it. It was telling me a story I didn't want to hear. I began to dress without looking at myself in the mirror. The night before, I had stuffed my men's clothes into my closet and told Abi to leave me to dress by myself. I would have to hide the breeches somewhere else, especially now Downall had seen me wearing them.

Downall did not challenge me about the clothes, or about where I had been. It was strange, and it made me even more on edge than if he had mentioned it. It hung between us, making me so nervous that I waited a few more nights before daring to take to the road again. The next time I rode the back way to the village, down the bridle path, glad of the meagre moonlight. I did not want to encounter Downall again, and kept looking over my shoulder to check nobody was following. I passed not a soul; it was as if nobody dared to venture outside. No ploughmen rolling home from the fields, no cows tethered on the common, no lights in the tavern. It was eerie.

I had my list of Diggers in my haversack. Only one person

had been paid, and there were almost twenty more to pay. Perhaps when I'd paid a few more, they would realise who their benefactor was.

The road was quiet. A merchant in a horse-drawn buggy almost leapt off his seat when I appeared before him.

'Hand over your purse,' I said, the pistol pointing at his face.

He threw it down on the road. 'Now get on your way,' I said.

Needing no further urging, he cracked the whip, and careered away. When he'd gone, I dismounted and picked up the bag.

When I took up the reins again, the bag hung from my belt, heavy as a turnip. At Margery Barton's house I saw she had a corn sieve by the door for feeding the chickens. I looked around, but saw no one. I emptied the coins into it and dropped in the note. Then I kicked Blaze on, back to the manor.

Two paid.

I pulled open the stable door, but took a step back. A glowing lantern swung from the beam above, and Cutch and Abi were waiting for me.

'Where've you been?' Cutch stood up from the upturned bucket where he'd been sitting. 'It's foolish to ride out so late. Abi was worried something had befallen you.'

'You've been on the highway.' I saw her eyes rove over my men's breeches, then down, taking in the shiny leather boots that were too big for my feet.

'What if I have?'

'Are you mad?' Abi said. 'You risk your life! Jacob came by. He's worried. He says folk already think you had something to do with the Gawthorpes' deaths.'

I shook my head vehemently. 'I know nothing of that.'

'I don't understand,' Cutch said. 'Why are you doing it? Surely a maid in your condition—'

I cut him off. 'So I can pay the Diggers. To make up for the fact they trusted me. Ralph wouldn't have wanted them to be treated so meanly.' I explained my scheme. 'It was the only way I could think of. Thomas is missing, and I get not a penny from my stepfather,' I finished.

Abi was mutinous. 'I thought all that was over.'

'I want to prove to them that I'm with them, not against them and—'

'Well, choose another way to do it,' Abi said. 'I for one won't be turning a blind eye to any robbery.'

'Why not?' Cutch suddenly broke in. 'If she's determined? We could help. It would be one in the eye for Sir Simon.' Cutch's face was alight with enthusiasm.

I took a step back, shocked. 'I don't need your help. I'll do this alone.' The last thing I needed was some do-gooder trying to help me.

Abi was staring at Cutch as though she had never seen him before. 'Have I heard aright? You want to help her?'

'If she is to do this, then she will need us. She's…, well she's…' He tailed off. He was looking at me as if I should say something, but I knew what he was getting at and ignored him. 'I say we help each other,' he said. 'Stand up for Ralph, and the Diggers' way.'

Abi whipped round to face him. 'Keep out of it, Cutch,' she said. 'The Diggers never condoned stealing! She's the one who started this, she should be the one to take the risks. Jacob says that highway robbers are the scum of the earth and should hang.'

'Jacob says. So it's all about what Jacob thinks, is it now?' I said. 'He's not worth your breath. He hardly pays you any attention, and yet you—'

'Stop it.' Cutch stepped between us. 'Ralph and I spent many nights on the road. I know what I'm doing. If Thomas is dead we will need to amass enough money to set up somewhere else, Diggers or no Diggers. She'll need somewhere when…' again he stopped.

'When what?' Abi asked. 'What do you know that we don't?'

'Nothing,' Cutch said, giving me a meaningful look. 'We could set ourselves up in business somewhere else.'

'Us? Where? What business?' Abi's voice was too loud in the small space.

'Bath, Bristol, some other big city. If I had tools I could set up as a wheelwright. You could help me, do the scrivening, the bills, and so forth. Kate too.'

I laughed. 'You're a useless wheelwright. Everything you make falls to pieces.'

'Only because I haven't the tools.'

He was stubborn. I could almost see his heels digging into the floor. I had to stop this idea before Abi fell for it.

'But I don't want you to help me,' I protested. 'I'm fine on my own. Why would I need your help?'

He sighed. 'All right. Say nothing. Have it your own way.' He turned slightly so Abi could see his lips. 'But don't forget, I was a soldier. You need me because I'm good with firearms. Because I'm a man, and a man's voice will do more on a dark night than a woman's can.'

Abi, who had been watching this unfold with growing disgust and disbelief, stood up. 'What about Martha? What will I do with her in your fine plan? Leave her behind? You're both like children. You just don't think.'

'We'd take her with us to our new life,' Cutch said. 'Soon as it was safe.' I could tell by the vitality of his movements, by the way he latched onto the idea that he wouldn't let it go easily. And that he was desperate to see the action.

'So you're admitting you'll bring danger here,' Abi said. 'And hasn't this house seen enough bloodshed?' She snatched up her cloak and banged the door as she went.

'I've known nothing but bloodshed my whole life,' Cutch muttered, 'so what's new?'

Five Diggers paid. This was the third time we had taken ourselves to this bend in the road, yet still I was nervous. The first two nights Cutch and I had relieved two wealthy tradesmen of their purses. They had been riding solo, and capitulated when they saw us, thinking us to be two armed men. Tonight though, my stomach was fluttering as if it held something trapped within, and my hands were damp with sweat. I turned to look over my shoulder. I had the uncanny feeling of being watched.

I glanced up for reassurance. It was a warm night, and light. There was a three-quarter moon lighting up the road like a ribbon that snaked away into the distance. A fine night like this meant more travellers on the road and more chances to try our luck. On the opposite side of the road, Cutch was waiting on foot. I could see the glint of his firearm, and the pinpricks of light from the buttons of his doublet.

A rustling behind me. I whipped my head round, but in the dark of the trees I could see nothing. I strained my ears to hear. 'I heard something,' I called to Cutch.

'Someone coming?' Cutch asked.

'No, behind me – in the woods.'

I saw the whites of Cutch's eyes as he looked through the trees behind me, still, listening.

'Probably just a deer,' I said. Though the feeling of unease persisted.

We waited another half hour and Blaze grew restless, anxious to be moving. I quietened him, then saw a dark shadow round the bend before us. Another lone horseman. I raised my palm at Cutch – our signal. One person on his own was a good target for us. The traveller was riding slowly at a trot, not in any hurry. From here I saw no obvious saddlebags, but we wouldn't know if he had coin until we stopped him.

I pulled the scarf up over my face and tilted my hat.

He didn't see me until I rode out before him, one of Cutch's pistols aimed at his chest. The horse saw me before he did and sidestepped, nearly unseating him. When he saw me, he tried to kick his horse on, but the horse seemed to sense our intention and shied, throwing up its head, eyes wild.

'Dismount.' Cutch appeared next to him, grabbing the reins of the horse.

'I haven't got anything,' the man protested, as he slithered down. 'Please, don't kill me.'

I had no intention of killing him, but I didn't want him to know that. 'Empty your purse,' I made my voice gruff and hoarse, kept the pistol muzzle out at arm's length.

The man took off the bag that had been slung over his shoulder. Now I could see him more closely, I felt sorry for him; he was only a young man, perhaps an apprentice. His doublet was serviceable, but not expensive. His eyes darted right and left, his hand shook so that the coins rattled as he took the purse from his bag. I dismounted, strode over, and held out my hand.

An explosion of sound.

So loud it made me reel away.

Everything seemed to happen like a slowly turning wheel. The boy keeled sideways, eyes staring wide, his mouth open in a shout I could not hear. His hands came up to his ears. But the side of his head had opened like a burst sack. The hands could not seem to find the wound, but the pouch of coins flew up, arced into the air, landing before me an instant before the boy hit the ground.

I was aware I had taken a step back, that Cutch was clinging to the reins of the boy's horse as it dragged him backwards, spooked by the noise.

A black shape leapt into the space between us, like a swooping crow, swept up the pouch of coins and made for the shelter of the woods.

'Stop him!' I shouted, but Cutch did not hear me, his hands were full.

The man was just a blur of black cloak, but there was a scent about him I recognised. The highwayman I had met before. I fired my pistol after him, but was in time to see him leap astride a horse. I got the impression of the other man waiting there too, a big black horse behind the pale trunks of the trees. A moment later another shot whistled past my ear.

Cutch, hearing the second shot, grabbed me by the arm and dragged me into the cover of the trees. On the opposite side of the road, horses trampled through the undergrowth, but the hoof beats soon faded.

'Shit. What was that?' Cutch said.

'Seems we're not the only thieves on the road,' I said. But I was staring at the body. A fine mist, like a smoke, seemed to be rising from it. It formed momentarily into the shape of a young man, his face sad and puzzled. I blinked, and the picture was gone.

Cutch loped over to where the lad lay motionless in the road. He rolled him over, put his ear to his nose listening for breath. He sat back on his haunches, shook his head. 'Dead. Poor fellow. He was going to hand the money over anyway.'

I was shaking with shock and my voice came out too shrill, 'What shall we do?' I asked. 'We can't just leave him here.'

'Sit a moment,' Cutch said, 'whilst I think.'

My legs were weak, I almost fell down. I watched as Cutch dragged the boy by the armpits to the side of the road. There was a dark wet patch on the road that I could not help but look at, like the tongue finding an ulcer, my eyes kept being drawn there. He was someone's son, I realised. Yet I'd seen his soul depart with my own eyes. Nausea rose in my throat.

'That's it,' Cutch said. 'It's all we can—'

A tremor on the ground. I strained to hear, but my ears had been deafened by the shots. 'Can you hear anything?' I said, scrambling to my feet.

'Horses,' Cutch said. 'More than one. Quick, we've got to get out of here.' He ran for the cover of the trees where he'd tethered his horse. My legs were like straw, would not work to my command. I ran for Blaze, who was grazing distractedly, a little way up the road, with the horse belonging to the dead boy. Blaze was pulling up hurried mouthfuls with his teeth. I reached for him but he skittered away.

'Here, come,' I entreated. But he ignored my desperately reaching hands.

Round the corner came four horsemen, cantering. I dare not stay, I ran into the woods. The two at the front were unmistakeable. Constable Mallinson and Jacob. I'd know them anywhere. I stumbled away from the road. I could not explain why I was dressed in men's clothes, why there was still the smell of smoke on the muzzle of my gun. I pushed the gun into my belt, leapt into the forest, running as fast as I could.

Shouts behind me. They had found the body. 'Fetch the horses,' Mallinson's voice.

'Where's the other rider?' another voice said.

I tried to move silently, creeping on the soft leaf-fall, taking care not to step on a twig.

Behind me I thought I heard my own name, but my heart was beating so loud in my chest I could not be certain. A branch knocked off my hat. I lurched back to retrieve it. My hair. No one must see my hair. I jammed it on, and crept forward through the trees.

A flash of tan and white. I let out a gasp and stumbled.

Just a startled fox. It ran for cover. But I'd made a sound, and they'd heard it.

'Hey!' A shout from behind. 'Over there!'

I pelted through the trees, uncaring now if anyone heard me. Panicked I dared a glance over my shoulder. A figure was weaving through the trees after me.

'Stop! Or I'll shoot.' Jacob shouted.

Over a tree root. Round a large oak. Heart thumping like the knock of the devil. Where next? There, where the trees are thickest. No hiding place. He was gaining on me. Don't stop. Think of Ralph.

He was right behind me, I could almost feel the thud of his boots. From tree to tree. Run. Give him no clear place to shoot.

The edge of the woods came upon me with no warning. I burst out, like a pheasant from its cover. Breathe. I couldn't breathe. Legs like lead. The open road, with fields either side. Nowhere to hide. I hesitated.

The ditch. The voice was clear as a bell in my head.

I did not have to decide, I threw myself into the ditch, under the shadow of the trees.

I lay motionless, the blood beating in my ears. The water seeped cold fingers into my clothes. I buried my face under my cloak, dragged grass and weed to cover as best I could.

I heard Jacob's boots land on the hard, packed earth and his breath rasp in his throat. Silence. I imagined him searching the landscape for any sign of movement. I dare not inhale. I sipped in air then held it.

A crunch of stones as he swivelled. His footsteps moved closer. Please God, don't let him see me.

A shout from the woods. 'Jacob?'

'Coming.' The footsteps moved away up the road, I let my breath out slowly.

'Anything?' Constable Mallinson, panting.

'Bastard got away. Lost him in the woods somewhere.'

'Found Katherine Fanshawe's horse wandering the road, but no sign of her.'

'Are you sure?' Jacob asked.

'I'd recognise it anywhere. Downall's got it on a leading rein. Maybe the highwayman's finished her too. Would solve a barrel load of problems if he had.'

'Don't, father.'

'Just saying, that's all.' The voices wound their way into the woods, drifting away from me.

So they wished me dead, did they? The cold seeped into my heart just as the water was seeping into my clothes. I waited until there was total silence before I sat up. I heaved myself to my feet, keeping to the edge of the road out of sight.

I had walked about a mile when I heard another horse. My heart sank. My powder would be wet and my gun useless. I had only a knife to protect me. I lay down on the verge in the shadow of a hedge.

Only when the horse was nearer did I recognise it.

'Cutch!' I hissed, still unwilling to make a noise. He turned; saw me. 'Get me out of here,' I said, in no mood to tarry.

'An "if you please" would be nice.'

But I was already climbing pillion behind him. I sat side-on, my hands around his waist.

He looked over his shoulder. 'When you and Blaze didn't appear, I was worried. I thought I'd better come back for you, in case…'

His eyes told me that he knew what I had been unwilling to admit to myself for all these months. 'There's nothing the matter with me,' I snapped.

My tone made him kick his horse on, but we still rode slowly back to the manor.

No lights were showing, so I guessed all the servants, including Abi, were in bed. He helped me down. I was shivering now with cold, for my clothes were sodden. The stink of the ditch hung in my nostrils. I was exhausted. A voice in the back of my head was telling me I had gone too far, that I just wanted to curl up somewhere safe and warm.

'Are you sure you'll be all right?'

'Just don't tell anyone,' I said. And it wasn't the highway robbery I meant.

14

THE QUICKENING

THE NEXT DAY I slept late. My body seemed sluggish, my stomach churned. I felt unlike myself, so much so that I could not bear to get out of bed. My back ached like the devil. I must have dozed because next thing, Abi was shaking me awake.

'Where've you been?'

I was still groggy. 'Nowhere,' I mumbled.

'You and Cutch weren't in your beds last night when I came up, and I searched everywhere. I was worried to death. I waited till gone midnight.'

I did not answer; just slid out of bed and reached out with my toes for my wool slippers.

'Kate, it's too dangerous,' Abi said. 'Forget the debt to the Diggers. Highway thieving isn't the answer. Aren't we in enough trouble—' Her hand clapped over her mouth as I stood up in my thin cotton nightdress. She looked me up and down as if she had never seen me before. Her face was stricken, as if with amazement.

'What?' I said. 'What are you looking at?'

'Your belly. We have had scarce any food these last months, yet still your belly is swollen.'

I looked down at my belly, rounded under my nightgown. Her words brought me up short. I placed my hands on my stomach as if to protect it.

'Your breasts too, they are heavier.'

'No they're not.' I said the words, although they sounded thick, like they were glued to my mouth. I hunched my shoulders, trying to look smaller. I already knew what she would say.

'And you've been riding, like a madwoman.' Her eyes widened, then narrowed into accusation. 'In this condition! You fool. Why didn't you tell me?'

'I was going to. I just wasn't sure…'

'A child. And you thought I would never notice? This changes everything. And Thomas missing. Doesn't he know you're having his babe?'

I shook my head. 'Not Thomas's,' I said.

Abi's eyes widened, her voice came out as a whisper. 'Whose then, Kate?'

I rubbed my hands over the swelling. It seemed impossible there could be another living thing in there. I looked up. 'Ralph's,' I said.

'Are you sure? Could it not be—?'

'No.' I bit off her question with my reply. 'I have never… not with Thomas.'

'But when did you… I mean—'

'The night of the rebellion.'

'Lord have mercy.' Abi slumped down on the end of the bed, and pulled at her apron with her hands. 'I can't believe you didn't tell me.' She shot me an accusing look. 'Who else knows?'

'I noticed the changes, but I don't know… I guess I did not think it could happen to me. I don't feel old enough… I mean, I still can't take it in.'

Abi was already counting on her fingers. 'The night of the rebellion…that's five months! Kate, you're five moons grown already! And you, still riding out!'

'I feel fine.'

Abi did not hear me. She could not take her eyes from my stomach. 'That means the baby will come in May. And then what will you do?'

'What do you mean?'

'If it's not Thomas's, what will your stepfather do if he finds out? Adultery, it's a sin for a woman. It will be the death penalty, or transportation.'

'Then he mustn't find out.'

'But he'll be back, soon as he finds Thomas. Even if he doesn't.' She backed away, as if she wanted to put distance between us.

I couldn't take it in. Nothing seemed real. But a part of me was rising up in jubilation. 'Aren't you pleased for me? Ralph's child. He will be your nephew.'

'I'm not ready to be an aunt.'

'It's a gift! So much sadness, yet Ralph will live on in his child. Come here, give me your hand, I want you to feel where the babe lies.'

I took hold of her hand and pressed it to my stomach. 'I can't feel anything,' she said, pulling her hand away. 'Maybe it's some other disease of the stomach. Maybe you're not having a baby after all.'

'No. I know what my body tells me. I just thought it might… that it might go away.'

'You haven't tried to—'

'No. Don't say things like that. Don't even think it.'

Abi's face was white, as if the blood had drained away. Suddenly I feared for my child with a visceral terror.

I grabbed her by the arm. 'Swear to me you will tell no one.'

She stood and backed away from me. 'Truth will out, Kate. How can it not?'

'You will not tell a soul. Swear on the Bible. It's Ralph's baby, your brother's child, Abi. Is it not a wonder?'

'It's a disaster,' she said.

15

AN INVESTIGATION

IT WAS REAL. The vomiting, the strange flutterings, they had all been signs. I was a woman, and hadn't even known. Ralph had taken over my body, just as he'd taken over my thoughts. Was this what he was trying to tell me? Sometimes I thought I could feel him watching me. It was too late anyway, to wish it otherwise. The baby kicked, as if it wanted to be heard. Already I could not imagine the feeling of *not* having Ralph's child inside me.

Abi laced me tightly to hide the bump because Downall was obliged to show around some more prospective buyers that had ridden from Oxford. I kept to my chambers, glad he was busy. I was dreading him challenging me about my riding out dressed as a man.

This time the prospective buyers were an elderly couple, accompanied by an impressively dressed footman and lady's maid. But true to form, as they toured the yard, my impression of Downall's demeanour as I watched them from the window was that they would not be buying. Not if he had his way.

As soon as they had gone I heard the doorbell clang again and male voices in the hall. Anxious, I brushed down my skirts and went down.

'Ah, there you are,' Downall said. The knowing look on his face made my mouth dry. 'The constable and his son have some questions for you.'

'Pray be seated. This might take a little time.' Constable Mallinson said. How stiff and self-satisfied Jacob looked, in his neat white cravat and immaculate twill breeches.

I turned to Downall with questions in my eyes but he avoided my gaze.

'We found your horse on the London road,' Constable Mallinson said. 'Last night. Running loose. It was only later we noticed that it was carrying a man's saddle. Did you lend your horse to anyone Mistress Fanshawe?'

I knew I had to keep my wits about me. 'No,' I said carefully. 'No one.'

'Then what was he doing loose on the road?'

'I've no idea. Perhaps he escaped my stable boy?'

'Cutch, isn't it?' Jacob said, with distaste. 'We will talk to him later.' Jacob had never liked Cutch. He used to be jealous of Ralph's friendship with him. It did not bode well. And the fact they were questioning me like this made me as alert as a hunted deer.

Constable Mallinson turned to me. 'So you did not go out last night?'

I hesitated, searching for the right answer, but before I could utter a word, Downall interrupted my thoughts.

'Lady Katherine was at home all night, Matthew.' He smiled at Constable Mallinson. 'I can vouch for her. I was here with her. Until late.'

I turned to look at Downall in astonishment, but he had deliberately turned away. What was he playing at? He hadn't been here at all. Worst of all, I did not want to be rescued by him.

'Are you sure, Jack?' Constable Mallinson asked, 'Because Jacob says he saw someone riding her ladyship's horse.'

'I couldn't be certain,' Jacob said. 'It looked like a man, but—'

'A man,' Downall seized on the word. 'Could have been our groom, I suppose. But I told you, the Lady Katherine did not go out all evening.'

Jacob was staring at me, and I hoped he could not see how I was shaking inside. He knew that I had attempted highway robbery before, a little more than a year ago. Ralph had told him, and in those days Jacob had been admiring, almost worshipful of my daring. But these last few months Jacob had changed, become bound in by convention, by the law. Would he tell his father? My hands grew slippery with sweat. I stood, and stroked my palms down my skirts. I could not afford to be arrested. What would happen to my baby if I was?

'Then you have heard nothing yet of the murder of a young man on the road – the brewer's apprentice, Will Pierce?' asked Constable Mallinson.

'I know no one of that name,' I said. Though my thoughts could not help but drift to the image of the man's soul drifting up into the sky and dissipating like mist.

'He's the cousin of the Sopers who own the hiring yard,' Jacob said.

'So? Half the village are cousins of the Sopers,' I said.

Constable Mallinson took a step nearer and pinned me with his eyes. 'Ned Soper says maybe he wasn't killed for his purse. Strange how the highway thief seems to target those who are most outspoken for Parliament. Soper says Will Pierce had no purse worth stealing, but he was ever railing against the King. Soper thinks it could be personal.'

He was implying the Sopers and I had history. My stays were so tight it made me breathless. I fought to stay calm.

Downall muscled his way between us. 'Now come on, Matthew, you know me for an honest man. I can assure you that we at the manor know nothing of any of this.' A few more persuasive words followed from Downall, and with each assurance, instead of relief I became more uneasy.

'Gentlemen, if that was all you came for, then I'm afraid we can't help. Sad for the young man, of course, but I'm afraid we're rather busy, so if you wouldn't mind...' Downall stood and with a gesture of his arms indicated that they should leave. I inwardly resisted Downall's use of the word 'we', but could do nothing about it.

Jacob looked disgruntled, but Downall had swiftly changed the subject. He was talking pleasantly to Mallinson of how his men were about to dam the river and flood the fields to irrigate them, all the while surreptitiously shepherding them both towards the door. The two men progressed to the hall and I made to follow them, until a hand took me firmly by the sleeve.

I turned. Jacob towered a good foot above me. 'You know something of this, I'd swear it on my father's life,' Jacob said.

'Leave it, Jacob. I know nothing.'

His eyes bored into mine. 'I know what you did in the past. That you turned highwaywoman. Ralph told me.'

'Those days are over, or had you not noticed? Ralph's dead. Why would I want to murder anyone? I've seen enough bloodshed.'

Jacob took me by the shoulders. His fingers dug into my collarbone. 'Take care, Kate. You may protest, but I feel it in my bones. You're hiding something. And it's my duty as assistant to my father to make sure the law is obeyed.'

I was hiding so much, the baby, my pact to pay the Diggers, but still I tried to laugh it off. 'Such pomposity! Where did that come from Jacob? Where is the sweet youth that used to sit on the hay wagon with Ralph and Abi for the meetings of the Diggers?'

'Don't talk to me of the Diggers. I was a youth. I've outgrown that nonsense now.'

'And Abi? What about her?'

A red stain crept up his cheek. He had the grace to look embarrassed. 'She surely doesn't expect—'

'Jacob!' Constable Mallinson appeared at the door. 'You're supposed to be interviewing that Cutch fellow.'

'Coming, Father.' He shot out of the door.

Poor Cutch. I could not warn him. Of course he couldn't have known that Downall had given me an alibi. I prayed Cutch would say nothing, but I followed Jacob towards the stables, intent on conveying a silent warning to Cutch. Halfway across the yard I was intercepted by the looming figure of Downall. He stepped in front of me, barring my path, a righteous expression on his face.

'Robbery's a sin. Thou shalt not steal, says the good book, as you well know. So if you value your freedom,' he said, his mouth twisting into a false smile, 'you'd best come within.'

My freedom. It was the one thing I was desperate to keep – for the babe's sake.

I should have known. The moment had come, as I surely knew it must. Downall was going to demand something of me for his sudden and peculiar cooperation.

As soon as we were in the drawing room, he turned to me. 'One word from me and you'd be arrested, you know that. I've seen you riding out in breeches and boots, like a man. Mallinson and his son might be naïve, but I know a lie on a treacherous woman's lips when I see one.'

'So what do you want?'

'I want your hand in marriage, and this estate.'

16

TWO ARRIVALS TOGETHER

I HAD GIVEN Downall no answer. What answer could I give? To refuse him would lead to more trouble. And the thought of accepting him was too grim to contemplate. I told nobody, not even Abi. From a child, this was always my way, to stubbornly refuse to face the things I did not want to see.

So spring came and my stomach swelled even more. I was so terrified of it showing that I hardly dared to eat, then suddenly I'd be faint with hunger and would have to creep to the larder in the dead of night. I had a strange urge to eat the dried peas for the porridge, and kept filching handfuls from the sack in the larder.

Downall had received written instructions from my stepfather in London that he must make the house look presentable for prospective buyers, although this was to be done as cheaply as possible. Downall ignored these instructions, no doubt thinking he would be the one enjoying the house in the future, so an army of carpenters and cleaners were engaged to repair the house, and sheep were found to graze the grounds. The ragged topiary was re-trimmed and expensive wool work curtains rehung in the principal rooms.

Downall was so preoccupied with overseeing his new empire that he had little time for me. Once he remarked that I was thickening at the waist, and my heart almost jumped from my chest.

'It suits you,' he said, admiringly. 'A woman looks better with more flesh on her bones.'

The twin emotions of relief that I wasn't discovered, and revulsion at his insinuation, flooded through me. Whenever I had to meet with Downall, Abi laced me so tight I could barely move, and I dealt with his business quickly, anxious to be free of the restriction and able to breathe once more. Finally as I grew bigger, I pretended such enthusiasm for an embroidered fire screen that I begged to have Abi bring my meals to me. From below I could hear Downall and his men drinking and laughing like lords, making themselves at home in my dining room. I resented it, but there was little I could do.

To all outside appearances the refurbished house looked grand enough, but it still felt hollow to me. For a Puritan, Downall certainly had ostentatious taste. I hated the gaudy furnishings, none of which were to my liking. I never rode out now or went to the village because I feared what jolting on a horse or in a cart might do for my growing baby. Besides, I did not want to come face to face with anyone who would see me. And to tell the truth I was feeling heavier and more tired.

A few weeks later, Abi was dressing me when she paused and stiffened.

'What is it?' I asked.

'Someone coming.' She'd felt the vibrations of the footsteps. Downall's heavy footfall stopped outside my chamber. The door handle twisted and he opened the door without knocking. I flung a cloak over my shoulders; wrapped it tight.

'I thought to see you at dinner,' he said, 'yet you deliberately ignore me.'

'I don't know what you mean. But if it is business, I will see you downstairs. Not here.' I could not keep my dislike of him from showing, but my tone was formal.

'Very well,' he said. 'I expect you forthwith.'

Abi drew my bodice so tight that I winced. Pray God it would not hurt the baby.

When I went down he passed me a letter. The words were blurred with damp, but they made my heart lurch.

'Downall,

There is no trace of Thomas in London. Worse, I have been delayed through this bad April weather with one of the main roads cut off by floodwater. I will get there as soon as I can. When I return, we'll see about giving you your own chambers at the manor. Mallinson speaks highly of you, and it makes me uneasy not having a man on the premises...'

My stepfather's florid signature followed. I needed to read no further.

Downall saw my stricken face and gave a half-smile. 'It appears we will be seeing a little more of each other,' he said, approaching uncomfortably close, so that I smelled the rancid tang of his hair oil. I recoiled, but dipped my head in the semblance of an agreement. I did not want to meet his eyes, or he would sense my defiance and it would rile him.

'Perhaps you will be a little warmer to me in future,' he said. 'Especially as when he arrives I plan to make Sir Simon my offer for the house.'

So that was it. I should have guessed. And of course by 'the house', he meant me too.

A hot temper flared inside me, sudden as a fire leaps into life. 'He will not sell to you,' I said, my control gone. 'He sees the snake you are. You have not deceived him, any more than you have deceived me.'

His hand whipped out and took me by the arm. His fingers pressed through the flesh to the bone. 'I know you do not like me, Katherine, but you will learn to.'

I gave a sudden twist and freed my arm.

'I would rather learn to skin a pig.'

I heaved myself up the stairs and into my chamber, grabbed a knife and jammed it into the latch to prevent it opening.

'What are you going to do when the baby comes?' Abi asked later that day when I told her Sir Simon was on his way.

I shook my head. It was question I had no answer for. Just like the question of what to do about Downall.

'I know you don't want to, but you've got to think about it, Kate. You might be able to hide a pregnancy, but you won't be able to hide a baby. You'll have to find a wet nurse, and then someone who will take him in. But it will have to be done quietly, so no one—'

I found my voice. 'No,' I said with vehemence. 'I can't give my baby up.'

'They'll kill you.'

'We'll just have to hide it.'

Abi looked at me dubiously. 'Where?'

'I'll think of something.'

'Then think fast. The buds are out on the May already. You're running out of time.'

'There's a whole month yet. Stop haranguing me.' I was short with her and I knew it wasn't fair, but I could not think what to do. It didn't seem real. These sensations I was feeling, the pressure in my abdomen, somehow I could not equate them to holding a real live baby in my arms. And I didn't want to think about it. Childbed was dangerous; many women did not survive it.

Weeks passed. I caressed my belly with my palm, soothing the child inside. Abi had brought some May blossom inside and put it in a vase. Though it looked pretty, the smell of it made me heave. I knew she meant it as a reminder, and I knew it was thought unlucky to bring it indoors.

Outside, the squally rain still hammered down, turning the yard to a quagmire. I shivered, feeling the cold, despite my layers of clothes. I wore a shapeless over-gown on top of my bodice. The laces would no longer fasten properly anyway. Over that, a fur-lined cloak. Winter clothes were good for hiding my secret. Without my stays my navel protruded like a button.

The babe inside me was restless, churning. I'd been out of sorts all day.

Worried, I picked up the stained letter from the side table, and re-read my stepfather's few blurry sentences;

I will get there as soon as I can.

As if to taunt me, a shaft of sun broke through the clouds, illuminating the room with sudden sharp light. So far, the floods had kept my stepfather away, but it looked like the weather was improving. I had to face it – Sir Simon was returning, and with me in this condition, there would be no hiding from him, that much was certain.

He would think the babe to be Thomas's, but that would give him more excuse to order me and own me. I would have to lace myself tighter, try to keep out of my stepfather's way, yet I knew him to be astute. He would not be easy to fool. I worried he would spot something amiss, and he was not beyond taking a rod to me, even now. Abi had been right all along; I must start to make plans.

I was about to open the door when a needle-sharp pain gripped my stomach. I stood stock still, and gasped for breath. And then it subsided. I told myself it was lack of food and hurried up the stairs and along the corridor to the tower where the servants' quarters were. By the time I got to the narrow stone steps I was panting. My legs seemed heavy, unwilling to move. I grasped the rope banister and hauled my way up, but as I got to the top of the stairs a sudden wetness gushed between my legs.

The baby was coming. This could not be happening. Not now. Not yet.

I burst through Abi's door, but another wave of pain made me clutch the door jamb with both hands. I groaned, and gripped the stonework, feeling my nails scrape into the grit.

Abi was darning a stocking but stood up, her eyes large with shock. 'No. Is it…?'

I could not speak, but she took me to her truckle bed and pressed me to lie down. I sat up again as soon as I could catch my breath. 'Sir Simon… what shall I do? He'll be here any day.'

'Never mind him,' Abi said. 'How long between bouts?'

I could not think. My back hurt. 'A few minutes, maybe?'

'Then there'll be someone here a lot sooner than him. Lie here, and for God's sake don't scream. I'm going for water and towels.'

'Don't leave me!' Suddenly I was terrified. I didn't know what was happening to me. A further wave of pain made me grind my teeth and groan again.

'I'll need cloths and you'll need something for the pain. Here, bite on this.' She folded a kerchief into a pad, pushed it into my hand and rushed away.

The grip on my belly seemed to abate, and I thrust my legs out of bed and began to pace, round and round the room like a prowling tiger. When the pain came I bit down on the kerchief, but the urge to scream out was overwhelming. I curbed it. Nobody must know. I held onto that thought, praying for the cramp to fade.

When Abi returned I was on my haunches, leaning against the bed. Sweat dripped from my forehead, my back felt as though it was squeezed by the weight of an anvil.

'Make it stop,' I wept.

For hours Abi sat with me. I was aware of her going occasionally and then her return, knew she brought a Bible and began to read to me from it, the words from Creation. But when the pain came she helped me to muffle the screams with her hands. Several times I thought I saw Ralph, and called out for him, but somewhere inside I knew he was dead, that he could not be in this life where my body was all too solid, straining, cursing, following its own rules.

Sometimes I fought Abi off, railed at her, slapped out when she tried to hold my mouth quiet, yet still she kept returning.

'Don't they ask where you are?' I groaned.

Her face looked down at me with its habitual puzzled expression as she read my lips. 'I've had to tell them I have a stomach ache and I'm too ill to work,' she said.

'Oh Abi. I have to push!' The urge made me cry out, but Abi bade me hush.

It was tearing me apart.

One last push and suddenly something slippery came from between my legs. I scrabbled to upright to see, and a baby, red and wet, squirmed there on the bed.

'A boy.' Abi's voice was a whisper. She stared in awe.

He opened his lungs and began to cry, a cracked, tentative sound as if he was unsure how to do it. I had a sudden vivid image of Ralph, standing at the foot of the bed, but I blinked and it was gone.

Abi watched the babe's mouth open with wonder. 'Is he loud?' she asked.

I nodded, eyes full of tears. I reached for him just as I heard the sound of footsteps on the stairs.

'The door!' I hissed. 'Quick! Someone's coming!'

'You all right, Abi?' It was the maid of all work, Nancy, from the kitchen. 'I heard a noise.'

'It's Nancy,' I mouthed to Abi.

The door creaked open, but just in time Abi leapt to shut it and batten down the latch.

'Hey! What the devil...?' came Nancy's voice as she shook the door. 'Let me—'

Abi could not hear her, so yelled over her, 'I'm not fit to be seen. I'm sick. I told them. Just leave me alone.'

'Stupid bloody girl. I can't talk to you behind there, can I? Whose cockeyed idea was it to take on someone deaf? Bloody useless.' With one final thump at the door her footsteps retreated downstairs.

'Has she gone?' Abi asked.

I nodded, but turned my attention immediately to the baby. 'We'll need to cut the cord.'

'I don't know how, do you?' Abi said, her eyes scared.

'No. And I'm afraid. What if we hurt him?'

'I know someone who will know.'

'Who?' I was immediately wary.

'Cutch. He's been a chirurgeon in the wars. It's either that or do it ourselves. And I'm not sure what to do. He's so little. Please Kate, I don't want to do it.'

'No.' I gathered my little son to my chest, terrified. 'Someone might see you or Cutch. I'll do it myself. I think I know what to do. But I'll need a clean sharp knife and some twine.' I mimed cutting and tying.

'I can't go to the kitchen, they think I'm ill. Where else?'

'In the drawer of the study. There's a knife for cutting quills and twine for parcels.'

'The quill knife?' Abi was checking she'd understood.

I nodded and sank back. Could I do this? Cut my son free with a quill knife? The babe was searching to suck. I let him find my breast. Softly the door closed as Abi went out. I looked down at the baby in my arms, at his soft downy head. A bolt of love shot through me for this tiny scrap that was part of Ralph and part of me.

I had so little, and yet God had given me such a gift. A miracle from nothing.

※

An afterbirth had come, which filled us both with a mixture of disgust and amazement. Abi took it outside to bury it. Half terrified, I had severed the babe's cord, with Abi watching me like an owl from the corner. And now here he was – a separate human being. His own self.

Pride filled me. I'd done it, all by myself.

In the morning I suckled him and swaddled him with torn bedsheets. Abi had brought them before going back to her duties below stairs. She looked at us as if the babe's appearance were a mystery she could not solve.

I called him Jamie. James Ralph Ferrers. I couldn't even bear the idea that the babe might be thought of as connected to the Fanshawes. I was Katherine Ferrers. My marriage had been none of my will – a sham when I was only twelve years old. I had never truly thought of myself as a Fanshawe. I despised my stepfather, and his nephew who had been forced on me. They had treated me like a beast.

And my son was Jamie Ferrers, not one of them.

I knew I could not stay here in Abi's room forever, but my chamber was nearer the parlour and if Jamie cried, someone might hear him. Once Jamie was sleeping I stood up. Abi had left me pads to wear, and clean clothes, so I struggled into them, aware of my legs trembling like shivering leaves in a wind. Somehow I must to pass through the house to get back to my room.

I crept to the landing and waited until I saw Venner and the men go into the study before making my move. I gathered Jamie up and set off down the stairs, one arm pressing Jamie to me, the other clinging to the bannister rail. At the bottom of the stairs I missed my footing and jerked, seizing the newel post to stay upright.

Immediately Jamie woke, opened his mouth and let out an indignant cry. The sound pierced through me.

'Hush,' I whispered, willing him to stop, but he did not. He howled in earnest, choking cries that tore my heart.

I heard the study door open. 'What the hell's that?' Downall said.

I ran for the side door, hurtled through it and closed it behind me. I could not go past the front of the house so I scurried out into the garden and burst into the stable. Jamie was bawling by now, and my own eyes were filled with tears.

'Hush now,' I crooned, desperate to make him quiet, 'Mama's here.'

'Guess he needs feeding.' The voice made me spin round.

Cutch was leaning over the iron gate at the horses stall. I froze, my arms holding the still crying Jamie closer to my chest.

'Best feed him, unless you want his noise to bring Downall out here. There's a place you can sit over there.' He indicated the empty stall with a wag of his head. 'I'll keep everyone out whilst you do it.'

I hurried into the empty stall, out of sight, and settled Jamie to feed. Immediately his cries stopped and peace descended on us both. I looked down at him. How could anyone wish such a tiny thing harm? Yet I knew Sir Simon would destroy us both if he found out.

'That's better,' Cutch said.

I shielded my naked breast from Cutch, embarrassed and ashamed to be in such a position.

'What will you do with him?' Cutch asked.

I shook my head, having no answer.

'He's not the master's child, is he?'

'How did you know?'

'I've seen the signs before. Years of seeing camp followers and their babes. And I know to heed my instincts, so I watched. Saw you grow bonnier and bigger like a waxing moon. But you said nothing and tried to hide it, so I knew it couldn't be the master's.' He leaned over to look down at Jamie's little face now he was sleeping again. 'Looks like his daddy, don't you, little man?' He reached out a hand to touch the top of Jamie's head. 'And just like his daddy, he's sure to bring trouble in his—'

But the sentence was never finished. The sound of hooves approaching and the rumble of wheels.

Cutch shot out of the stable door and went to look.

Moments later he was back. 'A carriage, four horses. And two riders alongside. They'll need stabling. It's not safe for you here.' He hauled me to my feet, 'Quick, into the fodder store.' He shoved open a plank door.

I threw myself into the fusty dark, Jamie in my arms. Just in time for I heard a commotion in the yard – hooves, and jingling harness, and men's voices.

'Oy, stable lad. What's your name?'

Oh Lord. My stepfather's voice. Just the sound of it made my knees turn to water.

'Cutch, sir.'

'Ah yes, Cutch. Get someone to help you get the carriage away. Let's look at the stables, see if they're fit for my horses.'

'They're fit, sir. Just swept.' Through a crack in the planks I saw Cutch clamp the bar to my door.

I shrank back against the back of the store, in the dim cobwebbed shadows as I heard my stepfather push his way past Cutch, and into the stalls. I was still as a stone. Jamie made a small mewling sound and I hugged him tighter to my chest. Sir Simon's bulky figure was only a few feet from us as he examined the stables.

'Seem clean enough,' he said. 'Get the matching pairs inside. My men's horses can go out into the upper pasture. Give them a long rope, there's not much fodder this time of year.'

Another small whimper. Tears sprang to my eyes. I clutched Jamie tighter.

'We've got birds in the rafters,' Cutch said.

'Well, make sure you get them into the pot. Don't want pigeon shit on my harness.' The sound of men's boots going into the yard. 'Any sign of my nephew, yet?'

'No, sir,' Cutch said.

17

ABIGAIL'S LIE

A FEW MOMENTS later the wooden bar scraped, and the door opened. 'He's gone,' Cutch said, 'but he'll be looking for you.'

'What will I do? I can't take Jamie inside. I'll have to leave him here.'

Cutch backed away, shaking his head.

'Please,' I begged. 'He'll sleep now he's been fed.'

Cutch sighed. 'Go on then. His pa would have wanted us to get acquainted. I'll find a box or something to make a cradle. But come back soon. Before he cries again to be fed. That's something I can't do.'

'I don't want to leave him.' I kissed the top of his head. 'It's just for today. I'll have to get him away from here, find a wet nurse… anything.'

'Won't be easy. Folk will want to know where he comes from.'

'You won't tell them?'

'No. But you'll want to see him and—'

'Katherine?' My stepfather's voice bellowing in the yard.

My heart thumped in my chest. We glanced to each other, and I hurried to peer from the window. I was just in time to see Sir Simon stride round the corner to the front of the house.

'Go! Now,' Cutch hissed. 'Quick, before he comes back.'

I kissed Jamie one last time and bundled him over to Cutch. I hitched my skirts and scurried into the yard. A few moments later I crossed around the corner of the house only to almost cannon into Sir Simon.

'There you are,' he said. 'I've been looking for you all over.'

I tried to calm my breath, forcing myself to listen to his words.

'Have you heard anything of Thomas?' he said.

'No. You?'

'It's strange. Nobody's seen him. Not on the London road, or the St Albans road. It's as if he just vanished.'

'Let's go into the house to talk,' I urged him. 'It's chilly out here.' I feared that Jamie might cry, and I needed to drag my stepfather out of earshot.

It took me aback that Sir Simon seemed genuinely upset about Thomas's disappearance. I hadn't realised he even had a heart beating in that barrel-like chest. I supposed Thomas had been like a son to him in the late civil wars.

In the house, he interrogated me as to where Thomas might have gone, but I kept silent. I dare not tell him of the moment Thomas had realised he was not the man of my affections; that Ralph and I were lovers. It was this that had driven Thomas away, more than fear of Downall's Roundhead rabble. The wounded look in Thomas's eyes had shocked me, despite myself. The naked expression of pain.

That afternoon the rain lashed down, and all I could think of was Jamie. I pretended to have some embroidery to do, but after a few hours I knew he must need feeding. Downall kept staring at me, as if he could sense something different, but Sir Simon was oblivious to my restlessness and distress.

'I'll just fetch more silk,' I said to my stepfather, who had spread out his papers over the dining table in the main chamber.

Once in the hall, I threw my cloak over my shoulders and pulled up the hood. Breathless, I ran over to the stables.

'Cutch?' I could not see him.

No sign of him, though the horses had all been fed and watered.

A cry from the store. Jamie.

I took off the bar and followed the sound to behind a large stook. Jamie had been tucked into a crate filled with straw. I picked up my babe and fed him as quickly as I dare, but knew I should not be gone too long or my stepfather would wonder where I was. I must behave as normally as possible, despite my shaking hands and dry mouth.

As I slipped into the hall again, Abi stopped me, eyes wide with concern. 'I saw your cloak was gone. Where is he?'

'The stables, in the fodder store,' I whispered. 'Cutch is taking care of him.'

'Thank God.'

'I'll have to move him though, it's too close to the house.'

'Perhaps Sir Simon will leave.'

'He has no reason to. Unless...' I had an idea. 'That's it. I'll encourage him to go. Tell him Thomas said he was going to Winchester, or Coventry, or York. Anywhere but here. The further away the better. York – it's further north. If he asks, you must say the same.'

Abi was troubled. 'Do you think it will work?'

'I don't know, but I've got to try something.'

✦

My night was restless. I had yearnings in the pit of my stomach, and tears came unbidden to my eyes. My baby needed me, I could feel it. In the end I crawled from bed in the dark and crept past

Sir Simon's door, down the moon-pooled stairs, and hurried out to the stables. When I got there Cutch was pacing under the light of a candle lantern, cradling a crying Jamie in his arms.

'He's a fine set of lungs, this one, and no mistake,' he said. 'Thank heaven you're here. I don't know what to do to get him to stop.'

I unlaced my bodice and put Jamie to the breast. He quietened immediately, and my body relaxed. For a moment all was quiet as the babe sucked.

Once he was sleeping, I turned my attention to Cutch. 'I told Sir Simon that Thomas had always wanted to make a pilgrimage to York. He was sceptical at first, and said he'd never heard Thomas speak of it, but in the end I persuaded him. He's desperate to find him and will set off for York in the morning.'

'Good,' Cutch said. 'I've a feeling the little chap knows I'm not much use as a wet nurse.'

I stayed as long as I dared, until the sun paled the sky. Then I had to leave Jamie again and appear at breakfast as usual. To my frustration Sir Simon's departure was delayed. Downall appeared in the dining room without announcement, and worse, he had Constable Mallinson and Jacob with him. They needed my stepfather to sign some papers of loyalty to Parliament before he could leave. I too was required to sign for my husband in his absence.

I ground my teeth in frustration. Our business in the study took longer than I thought, and the waiting was torture.

I rang for Abi to fetch more ale, then took her into the hallway. 'Jamie,' I gestured to make sure she understood. 'It's hours since he's been fed.'

She nodded. 'Don't worry, I'll go. I'll take some cow's milk and a dropper.'

The paper was signed, though I made my sign as illegible as possible. A half hour and a quart of ale later, and the men were finally ready to leave.

'Stable boy!' Sir Simon shouted, calling for Cutch to bring the horses. How strange he should call him a boy when he was a grown man. Cutch appeared leading out Sir Simon's big-boned hunter, and the Mallinson's horses. Cutch's face was neutral, but his eyes sought mine. He was trying to tell me something.

My stepfather was about to mount, when a wailing from the stable cut through the air. 'What's that?' He took his foot out of the stirrup.

My heart shrank in my chest. Cutch gave me a sideways look, like a warning. We all listened. But there was only the birds singing. Thank God, Abi must have quietened him.

'I thought I heard a baby crying,' Sir Simon cocked his head.

'I didn't hear anything,' I said.

'Nor I,' Mallinson said.

With an anxious expression, Cutch thrust out his cupped hands to encourage Sir Simon to mount. He winced as Sir Simon's bulk went down through his muddy boot and into his waiting palms.

No sooner was Sir Simon in the saddle than the cry began again. The piercing sound of a baby wanting to be fed. I willed it to stop.

'You're right, sir,' Jacob said, pausing with his reins in hand. 'There's a babe crying somewhere.'

'Whose infant is it?' Sir Simon turned to me.

'I know not, sir.' My voice was too loud and bright. 'Perhaps it's just the chickens roosting or…' I tailed off. Sir Simon was already dismounting.

Jamie's yells made my stomach clench into a small tight fist.

'I'm sure it's nothing,' I said, desperately, following my stepfather inside, clutching at his sleeve.

'Stay here,' he said, shaking me off. He put his ear to the fodder store door, then swung it open. 'Come out. Out. Now.' The noise of rustling straw. 'And bring the child.'

Abi slowly emerged. She was clutching Jamie to her shoulder.

I held out my arms to take him, but Abi shook her head, her eyes boring into mine.

'What is this child doing here, in my stable?' Sir Simon asked.

Abi said nothing. Behind me, Constable Mallinson craned over my shoulder to see what was happening.

'Why are you not at your duties?' my stepfather pressed. 'Whose child is this?'

'Mine,' Abi said. Her voice coming out with a hint of defiance.

I felt myself grow faint, my legs buckle. I grabbed the top of the stall next to me and yet somehow I remained standing.

'And who is the father?'

Abi stayed dumb.

'Speak girl.' He stepped towards her, raising a hand threatening to strike.

'No. Don't hurt them!' I cried, grabbing his arm.

'Stay out of this,' my stepfather said, batting me away as if I were a fly. 'You are too lax with your servants.' He turned back to Abi. 'Did you think to conceal this child from me? Do you think I am a halfwit? Well you can take your bastard brat and find some other dupe to take you in. Your work here is finished.'

I leapt to defend her. 'But it isn't her fault—'

'Not her fault?' My stepfather spat out the words. 'Whose fault is it then? I've said it before; you should be stricter with your serving maids. How can she do her duties with a babe strung round her neck? She can't. Such goings on under my roof – she can't even tell me who the father is.'

The stable door behind me opened. Jacob stood there, white faced. 'I heard it all. How could you...?' he did not know how to speak.

Abi dropped her gaze. Her face was brick red.

Horrified, I leapt in, 'Jacob, it's not what you think—'

'Then what is it, Kate?' Jacob's words cut through me. 'You knew. And yet you kept it from me all this time.' He strode towards Abi, his face set and white. 'You took me for a fool. I had my sights set on you and all this time you were... you were... whoring with someone else. You disgust me. I hope you rot in hell.'

Abi's eyes followed his lips. She had understood every single word.

Jacob was out of the door in an instant. When I chased after him I was in time to see him swing himself into the saddle and kick his horse on. He galloped away amid flying divots of mud.

What had I done? I approached Abi to try to comfort her, but Constable Mallinson held me back, his face full of scorn. 'Don't waste your sympathy on her,' he said.

Sir Simon shoved Abi hard on the shoulder. 'Go,' he said. 'You're dismissed. Take your bastard brat and get out of my sight.'

18

BLAME AND BITTERNESS

ABI STUMBLED AWAY, still mute, clutching Jamie to her chest. I wanted to scream, but my throat was stopped. I stood very still, my heart straining at my chest. I must not go after her, must not make a sound. If I owned up to Jamie, what would my stepfather do to him if he knew the truth?

'That girl was a bad lot from day one.' Sir Simon's voice was like a rasp behind me. 'I don't know why you took her on. Stupid girl's held me up. I'll tell Downall she's banned from the Fanshawe estate.' He strode off, slapping his cane against his thigh.

I ran down the road. Abi was already out of sight. 'Abi!' I shouted.

Silence.

Questions burst into through my head. What would she do? Where could she go? How would she feed him?

Cutch appeared at my side, panting. He grabbed my arm. 'I'll go after her. It wasn't fair. You shouldn't have asked her do that.'

'Don't blame me! I didn't ask her. I had no idea she would do that, I—'

'A girl's reputation is important. Word will spread, in the village. They'll spit on her.'

'Do you really think I want this? That another girl takes my baby? But if I'd stopped her, said he was mine...'

The break in my voice made Cutch step away, rub his hand back through his dark hair. 'Jacob called her a whore. How could he do that? Bastard.'

'He was angry. He thinks she—'

'Then he's a fool. Abi would never do anything like that. Why didn't you own up? Sir Simon would only think the babe was Thomas's.'

'If I'd confessed Jamie to be mine, my stepfather would smell something amiss. He'd wonder why I told him nothing of my condition before. Besides, no son of Ralph's will grow up as a Fanshawe.'

'Aye, suppose you're right. I'd not want one of mine brought up his way, where cruelty and bullying rule the roost. But it's not right, this.'

'D'you think she'll go to the vicarage?' I said. 'They took Martha in.'

'Can't see them taking her on there,' Cutch said. 'An orphan's one thing, but a babe out of wedlock...' He glared at me. 'You could have stopped her. Why the hell didn't you stop her?'

'Don't look at me like that. It all happened so quickly, once she'd said it, it couldn't be unsaid. And I was afraid for Jamie – he's so little. I can't let my stepfather anywhere near him—'

'Ssh. Here he comes.'

Sir Simon's footsteps closed my mouth. Cutch busied himself tightening the horse's girth again. The men mounted. I prayed they would hurry.

'When I return from York,' Sir Simon said, 'I shall expect the house to be in order and rooms prepared for our party. You will need another maidservant. As you cannot be trusted to choose, Downall will choose for you.'

'No, I want Abi—' But my words were blown away by the wind. My stepfather and his servant were already trotting away. We watched their figures grow smaller as they turned onto the road headed north.

I dragged Blaze out of his stall. 'I'm going after Abi,' I said.

'Wait for me. I need to come with you,' Cutch shouted as I leapt up onto the mounting block. I did not bother with a saddle, just grasped a handful of mane to steady myself, hauled myself astride, and kicked Blaze on.

A man leading a pack mule was just ahead of me. I pulled Blaze to a halt. 'Have you seen a maid pass this way?' I called. 'Short and dark, with a baby in her arms?'

The man looked me up and down, then hit the mule with a switch to move it on.

I kicked Blaze into his path. I was desperate now to know where Abi had taken Jamie. 'I asked you a question. Did you see her or not? It's important.'

'Aye, I heard you. But I've no mind to answer. I know who you are. Now get out of my way.'

Cutch by this time had drawn up and was watching. 'She means no harm,' he said. 'She's upset. The maidservant's her friend, and we're worried about her and the baby. Please, if you saw her, tell us which way she went.'

He gave Cutch an appraising look. 'Aye. I saw her. She was crying too.' He cast me a venomous look. 'No doubt she got laid off by her ladyship, like all those others from the manor. I called after her, but she'd no mind to stop. She went on towards Wheathamstead.'

'Elizabeth's,' I said, kicking Blaze on.

'Thank you friend,' Cutch called.

19

SISTERLY LOVE

AT THE SOUND of our horses the door of the apothecary's opened. Elizabeth stuck her head out, and quickly withdrew, banging the door shut again.

Cutch hammered on the door like he'd break it down.

'All right!' It opened a crack. 'She's not here.' Elizabeth kept the door between us.

'Where is she?' I leapt down from Blaze, prepared to squeeze the answer from her by force if necessary.

'How should I know?' Elizabeth took a deep breath. 'All I know is, she came here with her bastard brat, expecting me to take her in. It's not my fault if she's ruined her whole life is it? She could have been wed to Jacob Mallinson. She's fouled that up, and no mistake. She's addled, as well as deaf, if you ask me, and I don't want to be dragged down with her.'

'Where did they go? Tell me!' My voice wobbled dangerously.

Elizabeth backed away, clutching her arms tightly around her chest. 'I don't have to answer to you. Anyway, I told you. I don't know.'

'You turned her out, a deaf girl and a newborn baby? Left

them with nowhere to go?' I grabbed her by the shoulder, shouting into her face.

'Leave off! It's not my fault. Don't you come round here, shouting blame.'

'You heartless—'

'You dare to call me?' Elizabeth jabbed a finger in my direction. 'You've never shown an ounce of charity to man nor beast, if I had my way I'd—'

Cutch cut in. 'Which way did she go?'

'We had words,' Elizabeth said. 'I was angry, and so was she. She'll be all right, though. She always knew which side her bread was buttered. The father will just have to step up. She can go to him, can't she?'

'You don't understand,' I said. 'It's—'

'Which way?' Cutch loomed over her. He looked ready to strangle her.

'Up the ways,' she said hurriedly, backing away. 'The bridlepath.'

Cutch ran to mount up. Elizabeth took two steps out of the door towards me. 'And don't you talk down to me, miss high-and-mighty Fanshawe. All the world knows what you are – turning good folks out with no pay.'

I flashed a glance to Cutch, mounted Blaze and gathered up the reins. We turned and I set Blaze to canter.

Behind me I heard Elizabeth yell after me, 'Don't thank me then. I hope you rot in hell, the lot of you!'

But I was already turning Blaze and galloping into the bridleway. Blaze seemed to know the way; he crashed along the muddy path, kicking up loose stones. Suddenly I heard a sound. Jamie crying. I pushed on round the bend and saw Abi, walking steadfastly forward, hardly a few yards into the woods. She must have felt the vibration of our hooves for she turned, an expression of fear widening her eyes.

I leapt off Blaze and leaving him loose, grabbed hold of Jamie, hugging him tight to my chest. I sank to my haunches in the wet grass and loosened my bodice. The relief of holding him was so sweet. Jamie opened his eyes and his pale blue unfocussed eyes met mine. He screwed up his face, about to wail. I put my finger to his lips and he reached up tiny fist and closed it round mine. Such small fingernails. Like little pink shells. He began to suckle.

A surge of protective love shot through me.

'What are we to do?' Abi asked.

'I don't know. They think he's yours now.' The words came out barbed. The thought hurt in a way I could not explain.

Abi folded her arms defensively. 'I had to say that. To protect him.'

Cutch had dismounted. 'So what shall we do?'

Abi looked to me. 'Best leave things be.' She held out her arms. 'I'll take the babe.'

'No.' I said, holding Jamie tighter. 'He's mine. I should look to him.'

'But you can't keep him at the manor,' Abi said. 'Downall would soon winkle him out. He's better with me.'

I knew she was right, but I could not admit it. The thought filled me with visceral dread.

Cutch put his hand on my arm. 'Come Kate, it's done now. Abi saved you both.' He meant to be kind, but he could not see the turmoil that raged inside me.

'It's impossible,' I said. 'What will she do when he needs feeding and—'

'I can feed him a little cow's milk,' Abi said. 'I'm his aunt after all. It will be the best thing. Less risky.'

'No. Wherever he goes, I go.'

'And have half the county searching for you? Have you transported for adultery?' Abi was adamant. 'What good would that do him?'

'I don't know! All I know is I won't let him go.' I hugged Jamie tight.

'Wait. Calm down. We need to think this through.' Cutch sat himself down on a fallen log at the side of the track.

'And what business is it of yours?' His matter-of-fact attitude riled me. 'I never asked for your help. I gave you a position because you were Ralph's friend, but now Ralph's gone.'

Cutch leapt to his feet. 'Are you trying to dismiss me? Because I was never a servant of yours, or anybody's.' He thumped his chest with a fist. 'I serve myself and my own good conscience. You've got yourself into a mess and as far as I can see, Abi only tried to help you out of it. The sooner she hands that baby back to you, the better.'

Jamie's face creased and he began to cry. I jogged him up and down, but he kept on, his little face growing pinker and pinker.

'Look what you've done!' Abi cried. 'Just stop it, both of you. All this arguing! I can feel the knives in the air.' She turned to me. 'Kate, give him to me. It's not about what suits us, it's about what's best for Jamie. I'll take care of him, I promise.'

Still hesitating, I could see no way out of the dilemma. I trusted no one, not even Abi, I realised. Giving up my baby to someone else went against all my instincts. Besides, I did not want someone else to be mothering him. I held him close to my heart.

'Have it your own way,' Cutch said. 'Don't blame us when Sir Simon finds him, that's all.'

In my mind's eye I saw again the whip hanging above the fireplace, felt its stinging pain. Not that for my son. I took a deep breath, held Jamie out. 'There is only one place I can think of, where you could stay,' I said to Abi, as she took him, 'but you may not want to go there.'

'Where?' Cutch asked.

'No.' Abi was already protesting, but I spoke over her.

'Your mother's cottage.' I took the key from the chatelaine on my belt and held it out. 'I'm sorry, but it's the only place that has no tenant.'

'Don't ask me to go there. I couldn't. I couldn't sleep there, knowing that's where... that's where she died.'

'I like this as little as you do. But I need time. It's all come too quick.'

Abi turned away, rocking Jamie up and down, her mouth pursed. My stomach twisted with guilt that I had put her in this position. I could almost read her thoughts. That I should have planned better in the months before.

Cutch went to put his hand on her shoulder, to turn her. 'Perhaps your mother's cottage will be a comfort. It will be better there, than taking your chances in the village. You know, we went to Elizabeth's to try to find you.'

'What did she say?'

Cutch shook his head. 'News spreads quick. You'd best wait now until the scandal dies down. Keep away from the village and all those wagging tongues.' He mimed talking with his hand. 'And the cottage has been cleaned, so there's no trace now of any... unpleasantness. And it's far enough from the manor,' he said. 'You'll be safe there for a few days, and I'll come with you, to see you settled.'

I did not like this, the idea of Cutch and Abi taking Jamie. I stepped between them, put on my haughty manner. 'It will only be temporary, you understand. Just a few days, whilst I think of something else.'

Cutch lowered his eyebrows and jutted out his chin. 'Thank you. You could at least say thank you to Abi.'

His look was so belligerent that I swallowed my pride. 'Thank you,' I mumbled.

'Sign it for her,' Cutch insisted.

I went to Abi and patted my hand to my heart, miming the words.

Abi's eyes filled with tears. 'No matter. It's what friends are for.'

20

A GREEN SLEEVE

For a week I rode out to see Abi and Jamie. As soon as dusk came, and I could make an excuse to go to my chamber, I hurried down through the back stairs of the old priest hole, a narrow, stone-stepped passage that led to the library. I'd used it last year escaping the Roundhead rebels. From there it was a short run to the back door, and Cutch was usually ready for me, with Blaze saddled up.

Today, I rode the quiet way through the woods, glancing up at the moon shining through the branches like a half-coin as I kicked Blaze on, down the track to the cottage where I knew Abi would be expecting me.

The cottage was shrouded in darkness, with just a wisp of smoke from the chimney. Abi did not want to alert anyone to her presence there, because she had been told by my stepfather to leave Fanshawe land. So far Sir Simon had been absent so much he had not re-let the cottage after Abi's mother's death, and nobody had paid it any attention. The door was ajar. Abi could not hear anyone knock. I pushed it open and slipped in.

Jamie was sleeping in Abi's arms as she dozed by the tiny fire. The sight gave me a pinch in the heart.

At the draught, Abi's eyes opened, flaring with panic, but seeing it was me, she stood and held out the sleeping baby. I took him and sat down in the other chair, but Jamie did not stir.

'You've fed him,' I accused.

'He wouldn't wait. His face was red as an apple.'

'You know I like to do it myself.'

She sighed wearily. 'I know, but his little mouth was open, and he was yelling. Keeping awake to see if he needs feeding again is driving me to bedlam. And sometimes I don't know what he wants. I don't know how to do this. I watched Mother with William and it looked easy, but Jamie's different, he always seems to want something, and it's harder when I can't hear him.'

'It's not his fault,' I said. 'He probably just wants his Mama, don't you, little man?' He snuffled and sighed in my arms, fast asleep.

'You don't know what it's like. Someone might hear him if I don't keep him quiet, and it's hard for me because I don't know how loud he cries.'

'You should wait for me before you feed him. I look forward to it.'

She ignored me, as she did sometimes, pretended not to understand.

I leaned to touch her skirt, to get her attention. 'Look at him. He's grown though, hasn't he?'

'Pff. It's only been a few days. You imagine it.'

'I wish I could take him home. I don't want him to be brought up here.' I looked around the tiny parlour with its cramped walls and thin fire, and made a face.

Abi bridled. 'I was brought up here, and so was Ralph. It did us no harm.'

'But it's not what I want for my son. I want to give him the best.'

'But you always said you didn't care about wealth or fortune.'

'I don't. Not for me,' I said. 'But now I have Jamie, things are different.' I walked over and put him down gently in the cradle.

Abi stood up, her hand pulling on her hair, her expression worried. 'But you told Ralph you'd give it all up, join the Diggers. I thought you were all for the Diggers' ways?'

'I didn't have a baby then.' I turned so she could see my lips. 'The manor's his inheritance. What will he think when he grows up if I give it away?'

'You make me crazy!' Abi burst out. 'You can't have it all ways, Kate. I can't keep him forever. You have to let go of something. Don't you see? It's us or them. Sir Simon's way, or ours.'

'Do you think I like it? I don't want to hide him. I want to be able to hold my head up with pride and say, "This is my son, James Ralph Ferrers."'

Abi shook her head. 'Chaplin,' she said. 'Ralph was a Chaplin. He would have wanted him to be a Chaplin.'

I glared at her. 'But Ralph isn't here. He will carry on my family name.'

'What family? You have no family.'

It hurt, but I put back my shoulders. 'He is my family.' I looked down at Jamie.

'What about me?' Abi said. 'Don't I count? He's my brother's son, so we're family now, like it or not. When Jamie gets older he can still have a good life without all the trimmings of the aristocracy. Not a Diggers life, not the one Ralph would have dreamed for him, but still – a plain and simple life like the rest of us.'

All of a sudden I was overwhelmed. 'I'm lost Abi. I don't know how to be like you. I feel like I'm pretending, when I try. I can't farm, or spin, or churn the milk. But I know how to manage an estate, how to give orders and make sure they are obeyed. Those are my skills, Abi. You can't turn me into something else.'

'Then I feel sorry for your son – pulled this way and that, neither fish nor fowl. A farmer's son one minute, and a fine lady's son the next. Ralph was happy with simple things.'

Ralph. The name brought forth such a multitude of emotions. What would he think if he could see his son?

I blinked back hot tears.

He should have been here. Why did he have to die? The Diggers would have listened to him, I knew. Instead, my grand scheme to pay them back had hardly begun. Had they even noticed my gifts, I wondered?

'Don't you dare cry,' Abi said, her voice cracking. 'It's not so bad for you. Look at me and Jacob. He called me a whore. He'll never marry me now.'

Her words struck me like a blow. 'I didn't mean for this to happen,' I said.

'No. But you're like Ralph. Somehow you always make trouble.'

※

We did not mention the subject again, but I found it hard to eat for worrying. My body was scrawny now, my belly flatter than parchment. My ribs showed under my skin. One morning I was just dressing, trying to tighten the loose bodice so it would fit, when Downall appeared at my door. His knocking startled me.

'Jacob Mallinson's here, with Miss Chaplin.'

'What? With Abi?' My head swam.

'No, not that slut of a maid – the other sister. There's been another robbery, and a murder. Don't tell me you know nothing about it, because I know you do.' His chest was puffed out like a prize cockerel.

I backed away, wary.

'You have a choice,' Downall said, with a self-satisfied smirk. 'I can tell them what I know – that I've seen you ride out at night dressed in men's clothes. Or I can keep quiet.'

'You can prove nothing.'

'Oh, I think they will believe me, unless...' He let the words drift.

My stomach turned to a tight knot. 'What do you want?'

'I know you sent Sir Simon off to York. And I know as well as you do, it's probably a wild goose chase. Designed to prevent me pressing my case for our marriage. But the house is ready. I don't want to wait any longer – write to Sir Simon, tell him you think Thomas is dead, and to come home so that we can be wed.'

'No.' The word was a whisper.

'Then I will tell Jacob Mallinson what I know.'

What would happen to Jamie? At the same time I knew I could not marry Downall. What to do? I vacillated. 'No. I mean... wait. I need time...'

'Hello?' Jacob's voice from below, sharp with annoyance.

'Come, we mustn't keep the deputy constable waiting.' Downall gripped my arm and propelled me downstairs.

I took in the scene in a glance. Jacob's face was white and haggard. His eyes burned with enmity. And there behind him, Elizabeth, dressed all in black, grim faced, like his shadow. I did not want her in my house, and she knew it. Her eyes glittered at the sight of my discomfort.

'Where were you last night, Kate?' Jacob spat the words at me.

'At home, of course.'

'So you didn't ride out?' Elizabeth's voice was reedy in the echoing hall.

'No.'

'Show her, Jacob.' Elizabeth prompted him.

Jacob reached into his satchel and drew out something green. A piece of fabric with gilt embroidery and hand-sewn eyelets. A sleeve. I took a sharp gasp of air. I recognised it. My sleeve – one I'd given to the highway thieves on the night I rode out to fetch Mrs Binch.

'This was found on the road, near our house. Elizabeth says

it's yours; she's seen you wearing it. In God's name, why, Kate? What has my father ever done to harm you?'

I sense of dread crept up my spine. I heard my own voice as if from far away. 'Who? What's the matter?'

'Someone set our thatch afire last night,' Jacob said. 'Father smelled burning and I let him go out to see what was afoot. We heard a shot…'

I was already moving back, surely he couldn't think that I—

'He died on his own doorstep. How could you do that? Father had done nothing to you. Why Kate? That's all I want to know. Just some good reason.'

'I swear, Jacob, I know nothing.'

Downall sat down on the nearest chair. 'Your father's dead?'

'Was it because of the sequestration committee? You can keep your damned house. Just give me my father back. He was to teach me everything about the law. And then there he was, lying on his back with his chest split open. Or was it me you wanted, because I'm too outspoken against the King? If I'd gone to the door, then it would've been me.' His face crumpled. 'Why wasn't it me?' He raked his hand through his hair. 'There'll be no more words now. No more lessons for me on the letter of the law. And he'd only just started…' Jacob's voice cracked. He couldn't go on.

'You vicious bitch,' Elizabeth said. 'We'll make sure you hang for it.'

Hang? A cold wash of fear swamped me. What would become of Jamie then? I looked helplessly to Downall. His face was pale. He gave me a searching look. It was then I realised, he too thought I had something to do with it.

I dare not hesitate further, for Jamie's sake. 'I'm sorry Jacob, I'm sorry about your father… but Downall will tell you I was here all last night.' It was a gamble I hoped would work.

Downall stood, before his face broadened into a slow smile of satisfaction. 'Indeed she was.'

Elizabeth looked to Jacob, indignant. 'But what about the sleeve?' she asked.

'Sorry to disappoint you, Elizabeth, but it was stolen from me a few months back, by a dishonest maid,' I said, hoping my hot cheeks did not give away my lie. 'Why would I ride out and cast off a sleeve? I swear, I had nothing to do with Mr Mallinson's death. Someone is trying to discredit me.'

'Discredit? You discredit yourself,' Elizabeth said. 'You don't need any help from anyone else.'

The vixen. I glared at her, but she stepped behind Jacob.

'Come, Elizabeth,' Jacob said, turning to her and sighing. He rubbed his hand over his face, as if to rub away the lines of grief etched there. 'Happen I'm not myself. We jumped to the wrong conclusion. We must look elsewhere.'

'But it's *her* sleeve,' Elizabeth insisted. 'Ned Soper saw her galloping past. You don't believe her, do you?'

Jacob took her gently by the arm. 'I know you find this as upsetting as I do. Why don't you wait for me outside. I need to talk man to man with Downall.'

Elizabeth shot me a pointed look before she pulled her black shawl tighter round her ample chest and marched out.

'You're sure, Downall?' Jacob's eyes were glassy.

Downall nodded, but he looked discomfited.

Jacob bowed stiffly to me. 'I owe you an apology, Mistress Fanshawe. Kate.' He did not want to let go of the idea of my guilt, I could see it, but my eyes welled up at the sight of his attempt to be fair, to do the right thing under such circumstances.

'No matter, Jacob,' I said. 'It's a terrible thing. I'm truly sorry to hear about your father. Is there anything I can do?'

'I don't know what I'd have done without Elizabeth,' he said. 'It was such a shock, and she's been wonderful. She's helped me with Mother, and she says she'll help arranging the laying out. You'd never guess she's Abigail's sister. They're like chalk and cheese.'

'Abi's not what you think.'

'No. Enough.' He held up his hand. 'Don't talk to me of her. Nothing's gone right for me since I met her. And now this – a black cloud hangs over me somehow. She took me for a fool. The thought of it disgusts me. Elizabeth's right; Abigail always was the black sheep of the family.'

'You're wrong. Don't believe everything Elizabeth says. Abi's kind, and I can't tell you why… but it's not her fault.'

'She had a babe out of wedlock. How is that "not her fault"?' He shook his head in frustration. 'No. When Elizabeth and I are married, Abigail will never be welcome in our house.'

I took an involuntary step back. 'You and Elizabeth? You'd wed that simpering bag of air?'

Jacob's face was immobile a moment. He stepped towards me in a sudden rush. 'Watch your words Kate. You have few enough friends in the village. My father is dead. I'm constable sooner than I thought, and people will look to me for guidance. Elizabeth is a good match for me – she has the same values as I do. She wants stability, financial security. A decent life. Decency. Do you hear that? It's a little valued commodity these days.'

With that, he strode from the room. Behind him, the door banged shut.

21

STRANGER AT THE WINDOW

MALLINSON DEAD. It beggared belief. He was the linchpin of the community. No doubt Downall thought I really had murdered him. I could not help feeling a little guilty pride; that he thought me capable of it, though I knew I should not. Downall's lust for power made him prepared to ignore the fact his future wife could be a murderer. If it wasn't so frightening, I would have laughed.

But he had kept his part of our bargain, and I knew he would exact mine – to make me write to my stepfather. When I was sure Jacob had gone, I went to the stables and asked Cutch to intercept any servant sent to town with a letter to Sir Simon.

As I suspected, that afternoon Downall made me sit and write to Sir Simon, begging him to return. The servant took my letter and went to saddle a horse. From my window I saw him in the yard, and watched Cutch try to persuade him to hand the letter over. The servant would not give it up. Downall had outwitted me. He must have guessed I'd try to divert the letter.

Curses. Could there be anything worse? I'd summoned my stepfather home with my own hand. I gripped my skirts then thumped my fist down on the windowsill in frustration.

To my relief, Downall was absent most of the next few days. He rode out to St Albans and to Wheathamstead and offered employment at the newly refurbished manor to anyone lacking work. When I looked out of the windows, strangers were tilling the land, the kitchen was run by a new cook who called Downall 'master'. But I could do nothing, except keep my door locked and keep well out of his way.

When he left at night for his lodgings, it was as if I exhaled. My concern for Jamie meant I had to divert attention from myself. I slept in the day, an exhausted troubled sleep, for I rode out to the cottage every night to be with Jamie, only returning just before dawn.

I was jumpy, Jacob's father's death had shocked me. Who would do such a thing? He had been popular, Mr Mallinson. Staid and fixed in his ways, but well liked. The fact that someone could shoot a constable on his own doorstep suddenly made the whole world feel unsafe.

I armed myself well, and kept away from the edges of the woods, sticking to open ground. And I feared too that people would be looking out for me, would still think that I had something to do with it.

'Do you think your husband is dead?' Cutch asked me one night, as he handed me Blaze's bridle.

'I don't care where he is.' I shuddered; slipped the bit between Blaze's teeth. My thoughts had been so full of Jamie, I had forgotten Thomas.

'But you can't make plans for you and Abi until you know. What if he was to turn up here tomorrow?'

I stared at him. 'He's dead. No one's seen him. He'll be in a ditch somewhere with his throat cut by some roughneck Roundhead. Anyway, I've told you, it's none of your business.'

'But it is my business.' He stood up, from where he had been filling buckets with grain. 'You've lodged your bastard child on poor Abi, and she never asked for it. She's not your servant any more.' He took a step towards me, his face suffused with red. 'Sir Simon stopped her pay. The few scraps you took down to her yesterday from the big house aren't enough for what she does. She can't work, she can't go out. She can't do anything. It's not fair on her.'

'I should think it's an easy life, sitting around in her mother's cottage all day with nothing to do—'

'It's half a life!'

'And what do you think it's like for me?'

He had no answer. He threw on the saddle without looking at me. 'You need to leave here,' he blurted. 'Go somewhere nobody knows you.'

'Markyate Manor has been in my family for generations. It will belong to Jamie one day. When I am gone, and Downall and Sir Simon, and all those who would keep us from it.'

'Do you think your son will care a hoot about the house? He will care about who brings him up. Whether that person has time for him, whether they care.'

'Of course I care. Stop shouting at me.'

'I'm not the one shouting,' Cutch said. 'I lost both my parents to the plague. D'you know how that feels? I was twelve years old. My whole future disappeared. And guess what? I remember nothing about the house, not a whit. But I can picture my mother's face all right, the smell of her – starch, and the cinnamon from the baking.' He paused and looked down, his face reddening. 'Forget it, what I just said. But remember this – Jamie will care nothing for your fine house.' He spat then, at my feet.

The gesture shocked me. It was so much a gesture of the common man. 'My son shall have both,' I said stiffly. 'A loving parent and an inheritance.'

'Then you'd better start to work on the first.' Cutch glared at me and picked up the two buckets of grain to go to the stables.

151

'He thinks Abi's his mother. That's why he keeps bawling when you appear.' Two minutes later and he was gone.

Cutch's words had stuck in my thoughts like a fish bone in the throat. I loaded the provisions from the house kitchen into my saddlebags, guiltily squashing in as much food as I could fit. I would not have Abi think I was mean. I was about to leave when Cutch reappeared, stone faced, his horse ready saddled and bridled.

'I'll come with you,' he said. 'Abi needs some company.'

I did not answer. It irked me that he followed me all the way on his rough cob. It was still not quite dark when I got to the cottage. Abi went to walk with Cutch, to get out of the house. I could feel the atmosphere, sharp as arrows, as though they were both against me. They escaped me quickly enough, for Jamie was crying, and would not settle. I gritted my teeth.

'I'm your mother, little man,' I said, but he carried on grizzling. Cutch's words kept repeating in my head. I was a failure. I'd failed to win the love of my own baby.

In desperation, I sang to him, the Diggers' song.
With spades and hoes and ploughs, stand up now, stand up now,
With spades and hoes and ploughs, stand up now.
Stand up now, Diggers all.

The song brought back memories of Ralph, but filled me with pain. It was like being torn apart. Abi was right. I didn't know who I was anymore. I was two people in one body; I had the heart of a Digger but could not make myself act that way, Lady Katherine of Markyate Manor kept intervening.

My singing seemed to pacify Jamie though, and after I'd fed him and held him a while, he quietened, and his slow rhythmic breaths soothed me, and sent me into a doze. The fire was hot, ready for cooking, and the warmth made me sleepy.

A draught. I felt there was something wrong before I saw it. Jamie's eyes opened and he fell quiet, scanning the ceiling as if listening. One of the shutters had been pushed open. I shivered. I was sure it had been closed before. I had the prickling feeling I was being watched.

A rustling outside the cottage made me call out, 'Cutch? Abi?'

No answer, yet I could hear sounds of movement. The hens?

I stayed silent. A shadow, just a sense of a dark movement at the window. Then a pale shape. The eyes of a man. Looking in.

I jumped up, put Jamie hastily in his crib.

'Who's there? What do you want?' I called.

The door opened and a man stood there in the doorway. Too thin for Cutch. His eyes wild, staring at me, above a cloth tied over his nose and mouth. The highwayman who'd made me strip. Some sort of rage seemed to emanate from him, an anger that shimmered round him like a heat.

I fumbled for my knife, leapt up to put myself between Jamie and the stranger.

He ripped the dark kerchief from his nose and mouth.

Shock reverberated up my spine.

'Did you think I was dead?' Thomas's face was twisted in an expression of scorn. 'Well, you are not rid of me yet.' He was gaunt, his clothes rank and ragged, from sleeping rough. His eyes raked over me with contempt.

'Where have you been? We didn't know—'

'Is that the Digger's son? I saw you feeding him.' He stepped towards the cradle. 'He sure as hell isn't mine.'

'No,' I said holding the knife out in front of me to keep him at bay, 'don't touch him.'

'He's an ugly runt, isn't he?'

I shielded the cradle. 'Don't come any nearer.'

'You think you can defend him with that pathetic little knife?' He drew out his pistol and cocked it. 'My uncle was right when he told me you were a beast that needs taming. But I never thought you'd turn away from the king's cause.'

'Thomas, please, I never meant you harm.'

'But you never loved me either. How could you fall for that... that... farmer?' His words were full of scorn. 'You are my wife, Katherine. You were supposed to love me. We were wed in front of God. The same god that grants our king his divine right to rule. Yet you would turn to sin and damnation?'

'I followed my heart. What is so wrong with that?'

'Your heart. Pah. You talk like a common milkmaid. You were supposed to be my helpmeet, you were supposed to give me a son. Me, not that bastard Roundhead. Yet you barred your door against me! I thought you were just too young, that I should give you time.'

'Be calm, I beg you! I didn't want to—'

'Shut your mouth. You protest too much. You betrayed me. Look at you, look at this hovel, not even fit for a pig to shit in. Look at yourself Katherine – how far you have dropped. My uncle told me you were like him – nobility. He thought I was marrying up. I used to think you were too good for me, but all the time you were lifting your skirt for that—'

'Nobility?' My voice grew hoarse with suppressed rage. 'You don't know what the word means. Sir Simon Fanshawe has not one drop of noble blood in his body, do you hear? You dare to talk to me of his nobility, when he whipped my back red raw?'

'Because you were unruly, always have been—'

'What do you want?'

'To rid the world of poison. The world's got lost. Wives turn whores, and decent men like me are forced to live by their wits, preying on their lesser men, cast out from their own estates by men like Downall. Well, I'll clean up this rotten part of the world. Starting right now. Let me pass.' He pointed the gun at my chest and pushed me towards the cradle.

Outside, the noise of a horse whinnying. I backed away, shielding Jamie, my little knife held before me.

Thomas tried to push me aside, but I made a wild slash for his hand. I felt the blade slice through the cloth of his sleeve. He jerked back and the gun went off, sending a ball of lead into the thatch. There was an instant of silence, when straw and dust floated before me, before the door crashed inwards against the wall.

'Kate!' I looked up in time to see Cutch in the doorway.

I threw myself over Jamie to protect him. He let out a yell as if his lungs would burst.

Cutch had no time to prepare himself or draw a gun, but launched himself at Thomas. Thomas hit him hard across the face with the gun. Cutch reeled back, grunting in pain. At that moment a flash of understanding hit me like a fist in the guts. Thomas was no longer my milksop husband, he was the highwayman that had killed the Gawthorpes and that poor boy on the road. The man who had shot Constable Mallinson in cold blood.

Cutch grappled with Thomas, but I was too stunned to move, except to hoist Jamie up into my arms and get ready to run. But Thomas swept one foot swiftly under Cutch's legs, and Cutch fell heavily like a sack of grain. Thomas took the chance to barge past him, in a flurry of dark cloak, and out of the door.

Cutch pulled himself unsteadily to his feet. 'Who the hell was that?' He stumbled outside and came back holding Abi by the arm. 'I knew something was wrong when I heard the shot, so I told Abi to hide outside.'

'What's going on?' Abi said, her eyes flicking round the room. 'Cutch... your face? Is Jamie all right? I saw a man—'

I had Jamie in my arms and was pressing him tight to my chest. My breath panted in my throat. 'Thomas,' I managed.

'Who...?'

'My husband. He's still here. In Markyate. He knows about Jamie.'

22

HUNT FOR THE HIGHWAYMAN

JAMIE WAS in the old tithe barn at the back of the manor. It was draughty and cold, but a distance away from the house. I no longer felt he was safe in the cottage, and Cutch seemed to have taken both Abi and Jamie under his wing. I had not slept, because I had spent most of the night there, but lay down exhausted in my chamber at the dawn chorus. I must have dozed because shortly after the church bells had struck nine, Downall was at my door.

When I opened it, his bulk filled the doorway, his beard straggling over his broad collar. 'You'd better read this,' he said, holding out a letter, 'it's just arrived.'

'Why? What is it?' I got to my feet and took it.

'A letter to you from Sir Simon. Of course I opened it. It agrees to our wedding. He's telling you to put out the banns.'

I could barely think. The events of the previous night were tumbled in my head, the scene like something from a picture of hell. Thomas was alive. It changed everything.

'Try to look a little more cheerful over the prospect,' Downall said.

'There is no point,' I said with sudden satisfaction, tossing the letter down on the floor.

'It was what your stepfather promised me. Now your husband is dead—'

'Thomas is alive.'

He stared at me, stock still.

'He's alive.' I was triumphant. 'It is he who rides the highway. He who killed Mallinson.'

'Very funny.'

'I'm serious.'

Downall's face tautened. He took my arm in a grip like iron tongs, 'Is this true?'

'All the robberies, all the dead on the road – it is he who is responsible, not I.'

'Then I don't understand… why do you ride out at night? Are you protecting him?'

'No. I didn't even know he was alive until last night. But you see,' I could not keep the note of pleasure from my voice, 'whilst he lives, you cannot marry me.'

He stepped away, less certain. 'No. I don't believe you. You're a liar. Thomas Fanshawe's dead.'

I stood very upright and tall. 'Did you see him die?'

Silence.

'I thought not.'

Downall raised his chin, and his eyes glittered with suppressed rage. 'You say he is the highwayman. Then I intend to catch this highwayman, if it is the last thing I do. Then we shall see who it is that rides under the mask.' He strode past me to the door. 'And mark my words well, whoever it is, they will hang. I swear it on my life.'

As soon as Downall had gone, I hurried to the stable.

'Jamie's sleeping. Abi's looking to him. What's happening?' Cutch said. 'I've just saddled Downall's horse. He was in a mighty hurry to leave. He quizzed me over what I'd said to Jacob; whether I'd seen you abroad that night, the night Mallinson was shot. Jesus, Kate, it's a mess. I know where you were and what you were doing, but other people don't. They saw you. Riding out that same night. Of course I've told Downall nothing. Said I was asleep in the hayloft as usual. Told him the same as I told Jacob. I heard nothing and saw nothing.'

I shot him a grateful look. 'Did Downall say anything else?'

Cutch rubbed his hand through his flop of black hair. 'Says he's putting up a reward, wants the highwayman to hang. Don't understand why – he's always been lazy about fighting crime before. Is it because Mallinson's dead?'

'No. It's because I told him it's Thomas. He wants rid of him so he can control this estate. He wants to wed me.'

'God's breath.'

'But Thomas won't stand a chance, will he?' I said. 'Not once word gets out from Downall. Jack Downall can whip up a crowd out of nowhere. And Jacob will be right behind him, seeking vengeance for his father.'

'No,' Cutch said. 'It bodes ill, this manhunt.'

'Why? It will prove me innocent.'

'Think, Kate. It will be an almighty scandal in the county when Thomas is caught. Sir Simon's on his way home, expecting you to wed Downall. But once he knows Thomas is alive... well, blood's blood, and if I know your stepfather, he'll try to find a way to get Thomas off, and shove the blame elsewhere. And even if he doesn't, then Downall will still be there, waiting to take you to the altar. And Thomas is bound to tell his father about Jamie.'

'Saddle Blaze for me. I need to take a ride.' I had to get out of there. I was suffocating.

'Saddle him yourself. There's got to be an end to this. Abi can't give up her life for you.'

'It's not for me,' I shouted. 'It's for Jamie. Just a few more days, that's all I ask. I'll think of something.'

'A few more days might be too late. We have to get Jamie away, Kate. And if you won't come with us, we'll go without you.'

23

THE INTRUDER

Downall moved in that night, supposedly as my protection from the highwayman. A wagon arrived, bringing his trunks and cases and it filled me with despair. It felt as though I was shackled. I had to do something. They would catch Thomas, and then my secret about Jamie would be out. That morning a black crow had landed on my windowsill, and stared at me, its bead-like eyes full of knowing. It had felt like a summons, and I'd had the strange desire to follow it; to lift up black wings and fly.

With Downall in the house, it was a few hours before I could sneak to the barn, down through the priest hole. When I got there, Abi looked tired, her eyes red rimmed from lack of sleep. Jamie was awake and alert, wanting to reach out to take hold of one of my coppery ringlets and tug at it with his little chubby fingers. Cutch had given him a rattle he'd made – a wonky wooden handle with a smooth carved bone wedged on top. He'd drilled a hole and attached some tiny copper bells. When I waved it, Jamie reached out to try and grab hold.

'Look,' I said. 'He wants the rattle, but he doesn't want to let go of my hair.'

'He's going to be like Ralph,' Abi said. 'Not like you. His hair's coming through blond.'

Jamie finally managed to cling to the rattle. One of the bells immediately fell off and tinkled down.

'I'll fix that,' Cutch said, scooping it up. 'Just needs a better peg.'

Abigail smiled at him. 'It was a good idea, Cutch. Look, he likes it.'

Jamie's eyes were fixed on it, his face so open and soft. I didn't want to pass him back to Abi. I didn't want to leave him to go back to the house. My stomach churned. This whole situation couldn't go on, not now Downall was actually in the house, and deep within me lurked a growing unease, like a pressure building.

I could bear it no more. 'I've thought about it,' I blurted. 'What you said about going away. I'll get a few things packed this evening. Anything with any value. Then tomorrow, early, before Downall wakes, I'll take Jamie, and I'll set off for London. Nobody will know us there. I'll try to find some work. Do something…'

Abi looked to Cutch, questioningly.

'She says she'll leave,' Cutch explained. 'Go somewhere else.'

'When? I'll go with you,' Abi said.

'Both of us,' Cutch said firmly.

'No,' I said. 'Thomas or Sir Simon might send people after me, and I don't want to put you in an awkward position.'

Abi reached out a hand to me, and I took it. 'We're coming, and that's that.'

Cutch grinned. 'I'll have the horses ready. Bring a big cloth to use as a sling to carry Jamie in whilst you're riding.'

'You won't regret it,' Abi said. She took my arm and squeezed it. 'We'll start again. There's nothing to leave behind here, but bad memories.'

I found a leather holdall and filled it with some silver from the dining room, and with some essential clothing.

I stood a long time in the main chamber. It did not seem real that I would leave here and never come back. I could still see my mother, sitting in that chair by the hearth, her embroidery on her lap, the eyeglass hung around her neck, the soft creases round her eyes. She'd given up so much to keep this house for me, and I knew every carved rose on the panelling, every diamond pane at the windows. I went up the stairs slowly, my hand trailing on the smooth wood of the banister. I rested my hand a moment on the carved acorn finial at the top. I could not imagine myself anywhere else. A blessing or a curse, Ralph had said.

Perhaps it had been a curse after all.

Inside my chamber, I paced feverishly, jumping at every hoot of an owl. After a few hours of restlessness, exhaustion overcame me and I lay down. Instantly I fell into a slumber. Dreams of running, my feet stuck in mud, and then escaping, only to find brambles wrapped around my ankles.

My eyes snapped open. A rustle.

There was someone in my room. I sat bolt upright on the bed, ears straining. My first thought was that it might be Abi. I called her name softly, but there was no answer.

A dark shadow at the end of the bed. And the smell of smoke. Acrid, in the back of my throat. The figure moved feverishly, breath heavy and hoarse.

'Who's there?'

No answer. But the shape continued to move round the room.

'Be quiet.' The voice made my body turn cold, the blood seemed to drain from my veins.

'Thomas. How did you get in?'

'With a key of course. I still own this house. Or had you forgotten?'

As he spoke I slid off the bed, lit a taper from the last of the burning embers of the fireplace and held it up.

He cringed away from the light as I lit a candle on the mantel. It was then that I saw he was wounded. Blood had painted the front of his doublet with a dark stain. His face was gaunt, and purple shadows played under his eyes. He clutched his shoulder with an unsteady hand.

'Hide me, Katherine.'

'Why should I?'

'You're my wife. You'll do as I say.' His eyes were cold and glassy.

'No, Thomas. Please don't do this.'

'Move. Unless you want a bullet through the head. And then where would the bastard babe be?'

I grabbed a short cloak from the back of the door and fastened the frogging. I thanked God that Jamie was in the barn with Cutch and Abi.

Hoof beats outside the window. I turned to look out, but Thomas pushed past me and swept open the curtain. 'Here already,' he said. 'Don't open the door.'

'But what will—?'

'Hush!' Thomas clapped a hand over my mouth; pressed a pistol to my temple. From the corner of my eye I caught a glimpse of men dismounting in the yard, shouting to each other in the pale light of dawn, splitting up and surrounding the house. I saw the glint of musket barrels and pistols.

My first thought was Jamie in the barn. I had to get to Jamie.

Downstairs I heard the servants open the door, and angry voices in the hall.

'No, no one's come here, sir,' I heard the housemaid say.

'Then we'll search the place. Where's Lady Katherine?' the voice of Jacob.

'Abed, sir,' the housemaid said. 'Like most sensible folk.'

'Then wake her. That's if she's here.' Noise of jangling swords and boots on floorboards. Outside a horse neighed a high-pitched whinny. 'We three will take upstairs then, and you take downstairs.'

The clatter of heels on the stairs. Thomas grabbed me tighter, put the gun to my throat.

'Mistress?' The timid knock of the housemaid.

'Answer it.' Thomas pushed me forward. He hid himself just behind the door, the pistol trained on my head.

The heavier knock startled me even though I knew it was coming. I opened the door a few inches. Jacob Mallinson and another man in Puritan black were on the landing.

I drew myself up, and tried to be calm, though my heart twitched like a bird's. 'This is a fine time to be calling, Jacob.'

'The servants told me you were still abed, but you don't look like you've been sleeping to me.'

'I have many duties that get me up early,' I retorted, resolutely keeping my eyes from Thomas. He'd shoot if I gave him away.

'Would one of them include seeing to your injured husband?'

'Why so? I haven't seen him. You know as well as I do, he's been missing for months.' From the corner of my eyes I saw the muzzle of the gun glinting, only feet from my head.

Jacob was staring at me with hatred in his face. His complexion was waxy white, though smeared with dark smuts. My eyes strayed to his sword arm. His hand was black as coal, gripping the hilt of his sword as if he did not want to let it go.

'We shot a man on the road,' Jacob said. 'But he galloped off. A highwayman. There were two of them. Not only did they kill the publican from the Royal Oak, but then they set fire to the Binch's cottage. We couldn't save it. Nor could we save the occupants inside. It was terrible.'

'What do you mean?' My hand faltered on the door, and I glanced to Thomas. He raised his gun in warning.

'They torched the house. It went up like brush fire. By the time we got there the neighbours were screaming, and we couldn't get in. The heat... it was too much. It burned our eyebrows. We couldn't fight through the heat, though we tried. Like hellfire, it was.'

'Mrs Binch...?'

'Her and her son. They were in there somewhere, but none of us could get in.'

'God's breath,' I said, clinging to the door.

Jacob struggled to make the words. 'The neighbours said they saw them do it. Two masked highwaymen. One went right round the thatch with a flame. Johnson tried to stop him, but he hit him with the burning brand. Johnson's face is red raw blistered. Said it was Fanshawe – your husband. So what I want to know, is where is he now, and where is the other man... or woman?'

'No. Thomas wouldn't do a thing like that.'

I bit my lip. I was thinking of the old Thomas, not the man I had seen shoot that apprentice in cold blood, not the man who had tried to take Jamie. Not the man who even now held a gun pointing at my head. And who was the other man, the man who had remained in the shadows all this time?

Jacob lunged forward, took hold of my arm, his fingers sharp through the sleeve. 'Where's he hiding, Kate?'

I froze, praying Jacob would not see my legs quaking. 'I don't know.'

He grabbed my other arm, and shook me until my teeth rattled. 'Kate. People are dead because of your husband. They'll never come back, don't you understand?' He failed to control the quaver in his voice. 'I know you never knew the Gawthorpes, but my father... and Mrs Binch? She was such a good soul, and you should have seen the cottage, it was like... like hell. Tell me where he is. I know you're hiding something—'

'He's not here. That's all I can say.' I willed him to believe me.

Instead his face hardened. 'You Fanshawes. You're all the same. Stick together like shit to a stall. We'll find him, though. And when we do, I'll...' He shook his head, and with a sudden push, shoved me away, so I stumbled back into the room. 'You're not worth it.' He turned away from me to lope down the stairs. 'Search her chamber.'

I stood back, as Jacob's men rushed in, waiting for the shots when Thomas was discovered, but there were none.

'No one there, sir,' the man in black came out, and called over the bannister.

I rushed into the room, but he was right. There was no sign of Thomas. My heart sank. But I knew exactly where he'd gone. The old priest hole. It led out to the library. No doubt Thomas had made his getaway by now. I prayed Jacob would intercept him as he tried to take horse.

The men clattered back down the stairs, and I heard the front door bang closed and voices in the yard again. I hurried to the window, saw Cutch mount his horse and set off with the rest. So Abi must be all right, or he wouldn't have left her, I thought. I must go to them.

The house was suddenly silent. I was surprised that Downall had not been roused by the noise. Perhaps he had gone with Jacob's men too. I saw his door was ajar, so I pushed it open.

What I saw made me retreat back onto the landing.

Downall was lying on the floor next to the washstand. He'd obviously been shaving because soap was still lathered round his face.

But of the razor, there was no sign. And his throat was cut from ear to ear.

24

HOSTAGE TO FORTUNE

THE ROOM BEGAN TO SPIN. I put a hand up to my mouth. Had Thomas done this too? A noise behind me made me whip round.

The muzzle of the gun was at face level. 'You see, I don't forget those who swore against the king,' Thomas said.

I slumped back against the wall. So he had been hiding in the house all along. Cutch and Jacob's men were on a wild goose chase.

'I don't suppose you want to look on his corpse, so come with me now,' Thomas said. 'I've a carriage waiting.'

'No, Thomas.' I kept my voice low and reasonable. 'I did what I could for you, but I'm not coming with you.'

'Why? Because of the bastard babe? Grice will have him by now, and your maidservant too. It was his idea to search them out.'

The word was like an explosion in my mind. *Grice.* I'd thought he was dead. The name sent a cold wave of fear up my spine.

'What have you done with Jamie?' I shouted. 'Tell me! Let me by!'

He swayed slightly, barring my way. 'You'll see him soon if

you come with me. I see you're surprised. Grice and I have been working together. My uncle's weak; too ready to give in to Cromwell. But there's a whole network of men like us, men under cover, who fought for the king.'

Two highway thieves. I saw it in one swoop. The other was Grice. Now I knew, I wondered why I was so stupid not to have seen it before. That was why the man never dismounted – because of his wooden foot. Grice had lost a foot at the battle of Naseby.

'Grice has been coaching me on matters of survival,' Thomas said. 'And on much else for the Royalist cause, besides.'

'Let me past!' I launched myself at him and forced my way through. I ran for the stairs holding my skirts above my knees in my haste. As I ran through the hall, the doors to the principal rooms shut one by one, as the servants hid their prying eyes.

Across the field. Heart pounding. Feet skidding on the slippery grass.

I yanked open the barn door. 'Abi?' I shouted. 'Abi?'

I lit a candle lantern with shaking hands. There was no sign of Abi or Jamie. The barn was silent and empty. I threw up stooks of hay, hoping to see the small wooden crate Jamie used to lie in, but there was nothing there. It was as if they had never existed.

Frantic, I climbed the ladder to the hayloft – nothing. Down again. Empty. Out of the door. 'Abi!' I yelled.

'You won't find her.' Thomas stood quietly in the yard, pressing his wounded shoulder, his hand slick with blood.

'Where's my baby? Just tell me where he is.'

'The carriage is behind the hedge there, I suggest—'

But I was away, stumbling across the wet mud, breath coming hard in my chest. Feet tripping, half stumbling. A dark silhouette – the carriage; a boxy two-hander with one wheel askew. I slowed. I could not see Grice, or any sign of life. I was wary.

I went closer. I got to within four or five yards when I heard a baby cry.

'Jamie,' I almost wept his name. I covered the distance to the carriage in two bounds, dragged open the door and there inside were Abi and Jamie. Abi's face was white as whey in the early light. She was clutching Jamie, cowering back against the door.

Opposite was a tall figure leaning back on the leather headrest.

Grice.

'Katherine Fanshawe,' he said. 'It's been a while. I never thought to see any of the Fanshawes again, but then, I guess you never thought to see me either. Yet here I am.' He was relaxed, his bad leg crossed easily over the other. 'I'm like wheat, though, however often you cut me down, I spring up again.'

I tried to reach for Jamie, but Grice pushed his musket to Jamie's head. Jamie twitched but did not stir. He was too little to recognise the musket for what it was. But Abi cringed back. If he was to shoot, she knew she would die with him.

'This isn't necessary,' I said, my voice more measured than I felt. 'Tell me what you want.'

'You will come with us. If you don't, I shall shoot. Get in. Thomas will drive.'

'Where are you taking us?'

'I won't ask again.'

I climbed in. I'd humour him until I could find a way to get Jamie away. But what about Abi? I couldn't leave her with Grice either. My mind ran round in circles.

The carriage lurched into motion. I glanced to Abi, tried to catch her eye, but she would not look up. If the two of us could do something, maybe we could overpower him. But at the same time I knew the risk to Jamie was too great. We'd have to wait, bide our time.

'What are you doing this for?' I asked.

Grice smiled. 'For the future.' He leaned forward, his narrow eyes fixed on mine. I saw that his clothes were filthy, his beard matted. There was a deep cut over one cheekbone and the smell of him, like sour pond water, made me want to cover my nose. 'I don't matter, you don't matter,' he said. 'It took me a long time to realise it. What matters is the future of the country. That England should be under divine rule again, like it should be. You won't understand because you're still a child.'

'I'm not a child—' I began to protest.

'Oh yes you are, despite the fact you've somehow produced a babe of your own. You never knew the old days, when the king ruled and the land was at peace. I've seen men blown up by cannon fire, trampled by horses, their guts ripped out by musket balls. What were they doing it for, if not for a principle? They'd do it again if you asked them. Their ghosts stand behind me, the comrades in arms that stood beside me for the divine right and never made it home. If I give up now, what will it have been for?'

'What's this got to do with us?'

'You cannot be that naïve. You housed the dissenters, didn't you? You betrayed your class, you betrayed your God. You whored yourself with the enemy. You chose your side. Unfortunately for you, it's the wrong one.' He shrugged.

'What will you do?' Abi broke her silence. 'Where are we going?'

He looked at her coldly. 'Does it matter so much? Death comes to everyone. We are all only here for a short time, and none of us pray enough.'

I looked to Abi to see if she'd lip-read his words in the dark. She shook her head at me. She'd understood enough. It was then I realised we were dealing with a fanatic. One who would not be open to reason. An involuntary shiver shook my body.

The coach rattled on. Abi's gaze was fixed on the passing landscape. I guessed she was committing the route to memory. I tried to reach for Jamie again, but each time I leaned forward Grice nudged me back with the barrel of the gun.

The coach slowed and turned onto a rutted track. Through

the gloom I could see the stark outline of crumbling walls, rafters with no roof.

'Out.' The musket nudged me and I half fell out of the doors. Thomas was there with a pistol trained on the door. Abi passed me Jamie and for once, Grice did not object. We were outside a ruined house. I recognised it as Milbury House, the residence of Lord Milbury. I'd been here with my mother when I was a child, but then it had been a grand place with ornate plasterwork ceilings and chandeliers dripping wax onto parquet floors. Now it was clearly a ruin and uninhabited. With a sinking heart I realised nobody would have any reason to come here.

The two men hustled us inside into what had once been the main chamber, though now only two walls were standing amid a heap of rubble.

'This is what Cromwell's New Model Army did to Milbury's house. Low-bred louts, all of them. No respect for heritage or property,' Grice said.

'Serves well enough for a hideout, though.' Thomas said.

Grice ignored him. 'Here or Markyate Manor. What does it matter?' he said. He pressed us forward to the walls, and urged us to sit. We perched on dank stone boulders, our shoulders against the dripping wall. Thomas kept the muzzle of his pistol pointing at us; it was an eye that was hard to ignore.

'What do you want with us?' I asked.

Grice leaned back to ease his foot onto a stray boulder, whilst he kept his musket lazily propped within reach. 'They're hunting for us, and we know it's only a matter of time before we're caught. We won't leave the country, why should we? But I'm not stupid enough to think they'll let us be, and I want to maximise what we can do in the time we have left. I'll blast out as many of Cromwell's sympathisers as I can. Especially two-faced men like Downall,'

'Downall's dead,' I said.

'Yes. He wanted me to sign a paper to swear allegiance to

Cromwell. Bastard. I shook Downall's hand, but from that moment I vowed I'd have him, and all those other Roundhead dogs. I'd have slit his throat myself, but my damned leg is too painful for me to walk far. Thomas did the honours.'

Thomas smiled, as if it was a compliment.

'But now I need you,' Grice said. 'Thomas is no use; Puritans won't open their doors for him. But they will for you, so you will come with me in Thomas's stead.'

I stared, pulling Jamie closer. 'I don't understand.'

Grice picked a piece of dirt from his thumbnail before looking up. 'Tomorrow we wait. Until the hue and cry has died down. Then the day after, you will rid us of Owen Whistler.'

I opened my mouth to speak, but closed it again. I could not believe I'd heard him aright.

'He will open the door to you. You know them, all the Puritan men. One shot, is all it will take.'

'You're wrong,' I said, my voice shaking. 'Whistler won't open the door to me. We had a falling out.'

'Then you can go and apologise.'

'He's not a Puritan. He's one of Winstanley's men—'

'No difference. Did he fight for the king?'

'No. I can't—'

He overrode my words. 'Your choice. It is him, or your maid-servant and your baby.'

I tightened my grip on Jamie. He began to cry. Grice made a sudden move towards me and seized one of Jamie's flailing arms, pulling him away.

'Let go,' I said, clinging tight.

But Grice continued to pull and twist Jamie's arm until his little face turned red and he let out a piercing scream of pain. Grice was hurting him. I let go.

'See,' Grice said, dangling Jamie by one arm. 'I know what your choice will be.' He threw Jamie roughly into Abi's lap.

25

THE SHOT

THE NIGHT PASSED SLOWLY, and the next day was torture. The men talked in whispers, yet their faces showed they were talking about us. Grice was clearly in control, Thomas seemed to grovel before him. Abi and I shivered in the damp and wind, despite the protection of the Milbury walls. Once, Grice went outside to piss, and I signed to Abi to make sure she had understood what was happening, what he wanted me to do.

She was shivering with cold and fear. I told her not to worry. I'd make sure they were safe. Yet I did not trust Grice. His eyes were restless and his temper short; in this mood he was unpredictable – he might kill us all anyway, whether or not I did what he asked. Negotiating with him was a dangerous quagmire. Yet I still hoped there'd be some way out, some path I could take.

'Be ready,' I said to Abi.

'What for?' she asked.

'I don't know. Just some way out of here, some answer.'

She nodded, passing me Jamie to feed.

The next morning, dawn came too soon. I was nudged onto horseback, leaving Jamie and Abi in the ruins with Thomas. I did not want to leave them, but tried to act braver than I was. I prayed I would see them both again. I prayed Thomas had some ounce of charity left in his body somewhere.

Grice set the horses going as soon as a glimmer of light hit the sky. He had my horse on a leading rein grasped in one hand, with his own reins, and his other hand rested on the loaded pistol in his belt. My horse was a rangy bay with a roman nose, probably stolen from some other traveller. I bumped along astride, skirts showing bare ankles. At the village all was quiet, like a village already bereaved. The doors and shutters were closed. A few wisps rose pungent and grey, from chimneys that were still smoking into the morning.

Grice stopped outside Whistler's lath and brick house and told me to knock at the door. 'Don't try anything. Thomas has instructions to shoot them both, if you or I don't return.' He reached into his saddlebag and passed me the second pistol of his pair. 'It's primed,' he said.

My hand trembled as I fought the urge to turn it on him and shoot. But I had to hold back. What would happen to Abi and Jamie if I did? His pistol might catch me first. I wanted to hitch up my skirts and run, but found myself glued to the ground.

The gun weighed cold and heavy in my hand.

'Knock.' Grice's voice.

I mustn't do anything foolish. My hands were wet with sweat as I put my fist to the door. The last time I had stood there, I'd left coins in his churn.

'Who's there?' Whistler's voice.

'It is I, Kate Fanshawe, from the manor.'

'What do you want, waking me at this hour?'

'Don't come outside,' I whispered, my breath as close to the wood as I dared. I sent up a silent prayer.

Grice's horse came nearer, I glanced behind to see the pistol trained on my back. My thoughts were thorny, tangled like briars. If I waited until Whistler opened the door, and I didn't fire, Grice would shoot him, and then there'd be chance I could run... but no I couldn't. I still hesitated.

'Tell him to come out,' Grice said.

'I need to speak with you,' I called desperately. *Please, don't open the door*, I willed.

But the door seemed to creak ajar in slow motion, the dark in the cottage revealing Whistler in his nightshirt, peering out into the light with bleary eyes. He looked less imposing, with his bare ankles and reddened feet.

His face was hard and his mouth set into a scowl. 'I don't know what you want, but you're no friend of mine. Now get off my—' he began, but then he saw the gun in my hand and stopped short.

His words hurt. If he'd said something different, if he'd welcomed me as Ralph's friend, treated me civilly, then maybe things would have been different.

As it was, my finger was slippery on the cold trigger, and before I knew what I did, I closed my eyes. Fired.

26

DEATH AND DELIVERANCE

When we rode back into Milbury house it was drizzling with rain, and I was panting from the ride. The horse I'd been given was nothing like Blaze. It threw me from side to side with its uneven loping gait, and Grice was determined to gallop ahead of me. It was all I could do to keep up. I was afraid someone was after us, and afraid too that Grice would do something to Abi and Jamie if he got there before me. I rode as if the hounds of hell were both behind me and in front.

But I dare not think. If I did, I might realise what I had just done. I would not be able to bear myself. My limbs were chill, my mind blank. We clattered up the drive and I threw myself off. Abi and Jamie were where I had left them - it seemed like days ago. I hesitated, shivering. I didn't want to go near them. It might taint them, what I had done.

One look at my face, and Abi began to weep.

'I'm sorry,' I said. I dare not speak more words in case I should break down too.

'Come here,' Abi said.

'No.' I was ashamed.

'He needs his mama,' Abi said.

I felt tears prick my eyes. Abi went to pick up Jamie, put him into my arms, and enfolded us both in a fierce hug.

I turned to Grice. 'Let us go now. You have what you wanted.'

'And leave the task half done? No. This afternoon you will hold up a coach. Two more of Cromwell's supporters will lie in the dust.'

I said nothing. There was nothing to say, except to pray.

Before leaving I managed to get a moment with Abi, who was huddled next to an overhang to keep out of the weather.

'Kate,' she said, 'I asked Thomas how Grice escaped the night we tied him up and left him for dead.'

'And?'

'The Royalists thought that Roundheads had captured him, not us. They rescued him.'

'I wish you'd killed him,' I said.

'We all make choices in an instant. Choices we wish we hadn't made.'

Her words hung in the air. A vision of Whistler's face gave me a pang that made me twist my hands together. I pushed the image away. 'Listen. If the chance comes for you and Jamie to get away, take it. I don't care about myself. But don't take risks. And keep Jamie out of the rain.'

'Will you—?'

'I'll do what I need to do, to keep you both safe.' I kissed them both, before Grice told me to mount.

The waiting was the worst. The rain had stopped, but my shoulders were soaked. Grice gripped my horse on a tight lead rein in the brake of the woods. From there we overlooked the stony byway. Water from the trees dripped onto my hat. Two lone riders passed us and we had to retreat into shelter. I did not call out to them. It would have risked their lives. Grice would show no mercy, he'd shoot without asking questions.

Grice fidgeted with the reins, restless. 'Our man should be along any moment,' he said. 'He's stupidly regular. Returns from St Albans courthouse every week, at the same time. I tried to stop him last week, but he outwitted us. Came this road instead of the main highway. But if we can finish him, it'll be one in the eye for Cromwell—'

I had no time to register this information before he fell quiet. In the distance, the unmistakeable sound of a carriage. Crows flew up from the trees cawing, and wheeling overhead.

Grice pointed his pistol at my chest. 'Get down,' he said. 'Fire through the window. No mercy,' he said. 'Nobody to tell tales. Or your baby won't live to see another day.'

I slithered down just as two dark horses rounded the bend. They were pulling a closed carriage with an open space at the back for luggage. The back was piled high, with an oilskin covering the trunks to keep off the rain.

'Git!' Grice clapped his heels into his horse's sides, and it sprang into the road before the coach. A startled cry, as the horses skewed and the coach teetered and skidded to a stop.

A crack, and the smell of sulphur.

The coachman toppled from the driving seat, and the horses, panicked, reared up and tried to bolt. But Grice's massive gelding blocked their path, and the shafts prevented them going anywhere. I ran alongside the window, my pistol raised.

The woman inside was screaming, flailing, wanting to get out. The man struggled to restrain her. I pushed my gun through the window. The woman turned. It was Elizabeth. Her eyes opened wide and black with terror.

In that split second my stomach turned over. My gun faltered. I could not shoot Abi's sister.

My gaze swivelled to the man, but I already knew who I would see.

Jacob put his arms around Elizabeth to protect her. She closed her eyes, waiting for my shot.

Tears blurred my eyes. What was I doing? How had I come to this? I remembered Jacob and Ralph building their houses on the common, how they'd helped me because I was unused to such labours. They'd been building a better world. Grice had said I was on the wrong side. But in my heart I knew it had always been the right side.

I leaned in through the open window, determination making my voice harsh. 'Don't get out of the coach,' I said. 'Grice will kill you if you do. Stay there.'

Jacob's eyes were panicked. He ignored me, he was trying to open the opposite door.

'No, Jacob. Stay there!' I shouted.

But I had no time to think, from behind me another shot split the air. I turned to see the oilskin flapping and three men on foot running towards me. More shots. I suddenly understood. It was an ambush. A deliberate trap to catch the highway thieves. More of Jacob's men had been hiding on the back of the carriage.

Grice appeared behind me on his big horse, fired two shots at Jacob's men. Two of them fell. He gestured at Jacob and Elizabeth, still cowering in the coach. 'Shoot them, damn you,' he said to me.

'No. It stops here.' Another death in her family would finish Abi. I threw myself in front of the window, gun facing Grice.

Grice was raising his pistol again. 'Don't be foolish. Get out of the way,' he said.

I stood firm and braced myself; raised my own gun, cocked it.

Grice's lips tightened into a small hard knot. The black hole of the muzzle was pointing right at my chest.

I was about to fire when there was a flash, and at the same

time the carriage door slammed into my back. I keeled sideways. Grice's shot hit me like a whip-crack. A bolt of fire. My shoulder jerked back as if I'd been punched. Something white hot flashed in my eyes.

Blinded, I clung to the door. Shock waves reverberated in my ears. Jacob and Elizabeth were trying to get out of the coach. Grice went for his other pistol, but he was a fraction too late. I'd already raised mine.

I felt the slight resistance of the metal as I pulled the trigger; sensed the snap and release as it fired. The blast and recoil jerked my hand upwards.

Before me Grice swayed atop his horse, blood spreading a dark stain across his chest. He stared at me one long moment before his eyes lost focus and he toppled sideways. He hit the ground like a boulder, his wooden foot splayed out unnaturally to the side.

Another shot seared past me and I realised one of Jacob's men was still firing at me. Grice's horse reared and squealed. I shoved my foot into the stirrup and hauled myself up. The horse set off like a lightening streak, nearly unseating me as he leapt over something. I looked down, through motes of light. Grice's body was beneath us, lying spreadeagled in the road.

The rain pelted down in a sudden squall. My arms were weak. I could barely hold the reins. Grice dead. Thomas would kill Abi and Jamie. I would have to go back there, try to persuade Thomas it was not my fault. I turned the lumbering horse towards Milbury. Another shot. Shouts and running feet behind me. I did not stop, for the other men were on foot. On this big beast I could outpace them easily.

The rain lashed into my eyes. I knew only one thing, I must get back to Abi and Jamie. I turned off the main track, galloping through the rain-drenched woods until I came to the walls of Milbury. By now it was coming dusk, my skirts dragged on my legs; the world seemed wreathed in a kind of fog.

I slowed, preparing to tell Thomas what I knew. That Grice was dead, and that Jacob's men would be after us. I was ready to beg. When I slid down from my horse my legs almost buckled. I was breathless. I put my hand to my chest and it come away sticky. I lifted my hand to look. It was black with blood. A buzzing in my ears.

Staggering, I made my way across the rubble to the main chamber. The place was empty. In the hedges the sparrows busied themselves with their dusk twitterings as if it was any other day. 'Abi?'

No answer. No sign of Abi. No Jamie.

And no Thomas. What had he done to them?

I lurched from wall to wall, searched the whole place. It was then I came across it, the little bone rattle Cutch had given Jamie. It was trodden into the mud as if they'd left in a hurry.

I bent to retrieve it. The silver bells tinkled but it was a sad lonely sound. Nausea and hopelessness overwhelmed me. My knees trembled and I sank down onto one of the stones.

The rain had softened to a fine mist. Through it, a blurry figure was walking towards me. I blinked. Ralph stopped about a man's length from me. I heard his voice inside my head.

'You're going home,' he said.

The rain grew heavier and blinded my eyes, and when I looked up there was nothing but rain and the crumbling walls. Home. I grasped handfuls of wet skirts and went to fetch the horse. He waited whilst I stood on a boulder to heave myself awkwardly into the saddle. 'Markyate Manor,' I whispered, as if he could hear me, and set him to a canter. Perhaps Thomas had taken them there.

I was failing, I knew that. My fingers could no longer grip. My head weighed like a stone on my shoulders and I could barely stay upright in the saddle. I let the horse have his head and his hooves pounded through the lanes. The world was quiet, as if muffled. I was just aware of my head swimming, an icy coldness in my fingers, a pain in my chest like a red-hot brand.

I had to make it. I gritted my teeth and gripped with my knees, hanging on.

It was love I realised. That's what I was clinging to. Love for this life, love for Jamie, love for the feeling of riding in the rain. When the four domed towers of Markyate Manor loomed into view I thought they were a mirage. They looked so near, yet so far away. We seemed to be galloping, yet they got no nearer.

The reins slackened. I grasped a tuft of mane, but my hand could get no purchase. The horse slowed to a halt, but my body was heavy, unbalanced. I could not hold on. I fell, my cheek hit the wet grass, and the ground felt soft and welcoming, like a pillow.

I'd failed. I hadn't found Jamie. I tried to crawl towards the house, but my limbs were like water. I was going to die, and I'd lived a life in which I'd killed an innocent man, a man who would not let me be his friend. It was all I ever wanted, to have friends, to make a family for myself.

I groaned, let myself fall back on the grass. Above me the stars gleamed like pinheads just peeking from their cloth of black velvet. I felt something in me pulling upward, a stretching, fluttering feeling, like a butterfly slowly uncrumpling its wings. Below me my body was inert, the stain across my bodice blacker than coal.

Up I went until I was looking down from above.

Figures running from the house. Cutch was there, I could see the top of his head, he was shouting, shaking me. And Abi with Jamie in her arms. They were distraught, desperate.

I watched Cutch leave me and coil them both in his arms. Dear Cutch. It looked right. They looked like a family. The family I never had. It was going to be all right. They looked so heavy, so substantial in their solid clothes. And I was just a flicker, a movement in the air. But someone else was watching. A faint presence. Ralph. Though he was only a glimmer of warmth and excitement, like a blessing. I took one last look at the people below before I dissolved into love.

27
EPILOGUE

Abigail

Many folk have asked me about that night, and sometimes I don't answer. I pretend not to have understood, because it was a night full of confusion. People think I'm stupid, and sometimes that's a good thing. Of course Cutch doesn't, he knows the truth of me.

When I look back now, it's like a dream where I can't get things in the right order. All I know is that news of Whistler's death spread quickly, and fearing the worst, Cutch set off to search for us with two of the Diggers from the village, Ben Potter and Hal Johnson. Cutch followed the trail of the wagon – he recognised its wheel which was out of true.

At Milbury House, they surprised us, coming from three different directions. They were big men and armed. Thomas tried to seize me, meaning to take us hostage, but I was too quick and slipped out of his grasp. I took Jamie and ran and hid behind the wall. I remember Jamie's rattle dropping, and the feeling that

Cutch would be sad I'd lost it, but there was no time to go back for it.

Cutch fired twice. He missed on purpose, though he says he did not. Anyway, it was enough. Thomas was outnumbered and took to his horse. Hal and Ben went after him, but soon gave up. Their horses were farm beasts, not hot enough for the chase.

In the silence, Cutch took off his cloak and wrapped it about us against the rain. 'Better get to the manor,' he said. 'Can you ride? Tie Jamie in tight with your shawl, so he won't fall off.'

'Kate...?'

'She'll find us there, never fear. Out in this damp weather's no place for any babe.'

He was right. Solid, sensible Cutch. I almost wept with relief. As he helped me onto his horse, he took me by the waist. I looked into his face and it was as if I saw my name written there. I held his eyes a moment.

'That Jacob's a fool,' he said.

Four years on now, and the manor is sold. Of Sir Simon and Thomas Fanshawe, we've heard no more. Rumour is, they're exiled in France again, but in any case, they have no reason to return to the house now it belongs to someone else. Just as well. Bad blood, both of them. And I'll never go back – too much pain stuck in those walls.

I can see the towers from my window, and remember the first day I ever went there. How Kate sneaked up on me so I couldn't hear her. I thought her too grand to be my friend then, but now I know she was the best friend I ever had. Apart from Cutch of course. That man – how he lifts my heart. Still can't mend a wagon wheel properly, but Lord how I love him.

Cutch took over Soper's yard and now he is known all over

Hertfordshire for the gentleness of his hired horses. Cutch is a good husband and father to Martha and Jamie, and now we have our own babe on the way. I feel the weight of my babe inside me and think back to Kate, holding hers a secret all that time.

Lord, how I still miss her. She was one of those people who after she'd lived her life, you realised it was always going to be a short one. Funny how you can see it afterwards, as if you always knew. She and Ralph – both of them made more of sparks of fire than earthly body. Cutch says some folks are destined to live short, and burn bright. Me and Cutch, well, I reckon we're slow coals.

They say Kate's become quite a legend in these parts. Everyone loves tales of highwaymen, especially a woman, but I can't hear them so I keep quiet and let it grow. They talk of ghosts, but I'm too busy to be afeared of such things. It's the living you need to watch out for, not the dead. But I'm glad in a way, because Jamie hasn't much to remember his mother by, only these tales of daring and adventure. And a boy has to have something to dream of, that's for sure.

I look out of the window into the yard. Jamie's running after Martha. He'll never catch her, she's like a young colt, now, and his legs aren't long enough to keep up. She indulges him though, and she's good with the little ones, keeping an eye on them for me. As usual, there are two or three other children playing too. I recognise one of them as Abel, Jacob and Elizabeth's son. They've joined their hands in a ring and are chanting some ditty; I can see their mouths open and close in rhythm.

Cutch comes in to wash his hands before dinner.

'What are they chanting?' I ask him.

He listens a moment. 'Some nonsense about buried treasure.'

'Kate again?'

'Suppose so. They never tire of it. *Near the Cell, there is a well, near the well there is a tree, and under the tree the treasure be.* They reckon she buried a hoard somewhere hereabouts.' We laugh. He wipes his wet hands on my skirt. 'Though I shan't go looking for it,' he says, linking his arms around my waist. 'Reckon I've all the treasure I need right here.'

HISTORICAL NOTES FROM THE AUTHOR

HIGHWAY THIEVES IN THE SEVENTEENTH CENTURY

Though legends of highwaymen are many, there is only one featuring a woman – Lady Katherine Fanshawe. *Shadow on the Highway* is the first instalment in her story, the real history which over the generations has become embroidered with myth, as have all the other highway stories. Lady Katherine was supposed to have disguised herself as a man and her identity was only discovered after she was wounded as she tried to gallop away from the scene of a robbery.

During the English Civil Wars in the seventeenth century, many highwaymen were not ruffians at all, but well-bred men who had been dispossessed of their property. Sometimes they were Royalist officers who had no other livelihood after they were outlawed under Cromwell. These were men who were familiar with the newly invented pistol, which gave them an advantage over their victims, who were usually armed only with swords.

An example is James Hind, who held up the man who presided over the king's trial. A zealot for the Royalist cause,

HISTORICAL NOTES FROM THE AUTHOR

Hind intercepted the judge, Bradshaw, on the road in Dorset. When Bradshaw tried to intimidate Hind, he retorted;

'I have now as much power over you as you lately had over the king, and I should do God and my country good service if I made the same use of it.'

Hind became a symbol of resistance for the Royalists, and he continued to help the Royalist resistance in Ireland by supplying them with gold for arms and weaponry. Grice's behaviour in *Lady of the Highway* is based on men like Hind.

However, the first popular highwayman people think of is Dick Turpin, who is probably the most famous one of all. He is supposed to have ridden from London to York on his faithful mare, Black Bess, in less than a day. Like most highway stories, this is also a legend, probably based upon another seventeenth century highwayman, John Nevison, known as 'Swift Nick', who early one morning in 1676 robbed a sailor near Gads Hill, in Kent. In order to provide himself with an alibi, Nevison apparently set off on a ride that took him more than a hundred and ninety miles in about fifteen hours. Nevinson was a Robin Hood-type character, who would redistribute his takings to the poor.

> Now when I rode on the highway,
> I always had money in store,
> And whatever I took from the rich
> Why I freely gave it to the poor.
> *from the ballad 'Bold Nevison'*

Dick Turpin, on the other hand was a ruthless, violent character known to many as 'Turpin the Butcher'. Not the romantic hero we would like to remember. A much more dashing figure altogether was the Frenchman, Claude Du Vall.

> Here lies Du Vall, Reader, if male thou art,
> Look to thy purse. If female, to thy heart.

HISTORICAL NOTES FROM THE AUTHOR

> Much havoc has he made of both; for all
> Men he made to stand, and women he made to fall
> The second Conqueror of the Norman race,
> Knights to his arm did yield, and ladies to his face.
> Old Tyburn's glory; England's illustrious Thief,
> Du Vall, the ladies' joy; Du Vall, the ladies' grief.
> *from his memorial in St Paul's, Covent Garden*

Du Vall was born in Normandy in 1643 to a family of millers, but later found work as a stable boy in Rouen, where he was hired by a group of English Royalists to look after their horses. He followed them back to England when Charles II was restored to the throne. By 1666 he was mentioned by name as a highwayman, though he was well dressed and well mannered, and never used violence on his victims. Du Vall soon became a popular icon with the ladies, who thought him gallant and daring. His haunts included the northern approaches to London, especially Hounslow Heath.

Perhaps because they concentrated on the wealthy, highwaymen became popular heroes. Claude Du Vall only added to his notoriety when he danced with a beautiful victim on the heath and then let her wealthy husband go free for a purse of a hundred pounds. A Victorian picture by Frith shows the scene, including the companion in the coach who has fainted away with the shock!

It was a treat to write about highway robbery from a girl's point of view, and to imagine the anticipation of listening for that coach to rumble up the highway.

Ralph Chaplin and the Real Lady Katherine Fanshawe (The Wicked Lady)

Lady Katherine Fanshawe really did exist. Katherine was born on 4th May 1634 into a wealthy family, the Ferrers. Tragically, her father, Knighton Ferrers, died two weeks before she was born, and her grandfather shortly after, leaving her the sole heir to a fortune.

A few years later her mother was married again, to the spendthrift and gambler Sir Simon Fanshawe. Unfortunately, Katherine's mother died when she was only eight, leaving her at the mercy of the Fanshawe family. Sir Simon supported the Royalist cause and the king needed money to fund his army. Sir Simon conceived of a plan to marry off his nephew, Thomas Fanshawe, to the rich heiress, thus gaining control over Katherine's wealth and land.

During much of the English Civil War, Katherine's uncle and husband were away fighting, and spent much of the latter part of the war in exile in France. Whilst researching this trilogy, the stories about Lady Katherine that I found really fascinating were the reports of her exploits as a notorious highwaywoman. What went on during her husband's absence that would lead her to do the things she did? I decided there must be a long history, and that the answer could not be as simplistic as a lust for excitement.

There are no historical records about Ralph Chaplin, although his name always appears in the stories. He is widely believed to have been Lady Katherine's lover, and to have been a farmer's son who turned to highway robbery. He was tried and hanged for the crime. Other than that, little is known of him, and I could find no archival records for his existence. That being the case, I have taken the liberty of giving him a fictional family, including a deaf sister called Abigail, and a whole book to himself, *Spirit of the Highway*. Whilst researching this last book in the trilogy, I took into account both the real history of the events of the English Civil War, and the legend of The Wicked Lady. I also discovered that Lady Ann Fanshawe, Kate's aunt, wrote a diary, and I used this valuable insight into the period as part of my research.

Lady Katherine Fanshawe (Kate), Ralph Chaplin and his sister

HISTORICAL NOTES FROM THE AUTHOR

Abigail also appear in my earlier books, *Shadow on the Highway* (Abigail's story) and *Spirit of the Highway* (Ralph's story).

The Diggers were the first group of people to try and live in what we would nowadays call a commune. Led by Gerrard Winstanley, the movement began in Cobham, England, in 1649, but rapidly spread to other parishes in the southern area of England.

THE DIGGERS

The name 'The Diggers' came from Winstanley's belief that the earth was made to be 'a common treasury for all', and that all should be able to dig it, and provide themselves with what was necessary for human survival – food, warmth and shelter. The Diggers consisted mostly of poorer families that had no land of their own. They took over common land which was not already used, and began to cultivate it. They did not believe in enclosing the land, or separating one part of the earth from another.

Rich landowners found these ideas threatening, and organised men to destroy the Diggers' homes and ruin their crops in an effort to drive them off the land. The Diggers made several unsuccessful attempts to build houses in different locations, but were suppressed by the landowning classes and dispersed by force, and the communities wiped out.

Although the Diggers were a short-lived movement, their ideas had a far-reaching effect, sowing the seeds of communal living and self-sufficiency for future generations. There is still a Diggers Festival every year in Wigan in England, where Winstanley was born.

ROUNDHEADS AND CAVALIERS

In the middle of the seventeenth century, England went to war – not with another country, but with itself. This was a war which came and went, with brief periods of peace between each bout of fighting. It spread to Scotland, Wales and Ireland and to all levels of society. The dispute was one in which both men and women were prepared to take sides on matters of principle, and fight for their beliefs to the death.

In simple terms, the war was one between the king and his followers – the King's Army, and Parliament on the other – The New Model Army, led by Cromwell. Sometimes these groups are known as Cavaliers and Roundheads. 'Cavalier' from the Spanish, *caballero*, originally meant a mounted soldier, but came to be used as an insult to denote someone who would put themselves above their station. 'Roundhead' was a term used to describe the short-haired apprentices who first came out in favour of Parliament.

The fighting was over matters of political policy, and on how Britain should be governed. The differences between the two factions were complicated by their opposing religious views; the Anglicanism of the king versus the Puritanism of Cromwell's men. The war began when the port of Hull refused to open its gates to the king, and in 1642 the king proclaimed war on his rebellious subjects.

The English Civil War killed about two hundred thousand people, almost four percent of the population, and brought disease and famine in its wake. It divided families and stripped the land of food and wealth, as troops rampaged the countryside foraging and plundering whatever they could find.

Towns were flattened, and communities dispersed. For example, records show that Parliamentary troops blew up more than two hundred houses at Leicester just to provide a clear line of fire, whilst four hundred more were destroyed at Worcester and another two hundred at Faringdon.

There were nearly ten years of fighting and unrest. Some children barely knew their fathers as they had been away in the wars for most of that time. In effect there were three main periods of fighting, and this book is set just after the wars are over, when the king had been finally routed by Cromwell's increasingly efficient New Model Army.

The seventeenth century saw a king executed, followed by the establishment of a military dictatorship under Cromwell. It was also a time that transformed society, and gave birth to new ideas about political and religious liberty, as demonstrated by the Diggers and sundry other sects with alternative or utopian ideals.

ACKNOWLEDGMENTS

Thank you to Peter, James, Fiona, Robert, and John who were my early test readers.

I am grateful to the following books which, among many others, formed the bedrock of my research:

The English Civil Wars – Maurice Ashley
Going to the Wars – Charles Carlton
Brave Community (*The Diggers*) – John Gurney
The English Civil War at First Hand – Tristram Hunt

Thank you for choosing *Lady of the Highway*. If you have enjoyed it, please consider leaving a brief online review.

Reviews are gold dust to an author, and help more readers to find my books. And I'm always happy to chat to readers about books or history! You can find me on Twitter @swiftstory, or sign up for free special offers on my website www.deborahswift.com, where I also blog about history and historical fiction.

MEET THE AUTHOR

DEBORAH SWIFT used to be a set and costume designer for theatre and TV. She is the award-winning author of fifteen historical novels to date. She enjoys the research aspect of creating historical fiction, something she loved doing as a scenographer. She likes to write about extraordinary characters set against the background of real historical events.

Deborah lives on the edge of the Lake District in England, an area made famous by the Romantic Poets such as Wordsworth and Coleridge. When not writing, Deborah mentors other writers through The History Quill. She is a member of the Historical Writers Association and the Historical Novel Society.

FROM DEBORAH - CLAIM A FREE STORY!

Do join my community of readers via my website www.deborahswift.com or subscribe to my newsletter, The Astonishing Past. Newsletters are once a month and feature interesting snippets from our astonishing past and bargain books. A free story when you sign up!
GET MY STORY

ALSO BY DEBORAH SWIFT

In this series:
Shadow on the Highway
Spirit of the Highway

The Poison Keeper
A Divided Inheritance
The Lady's Slipper
The Gilded Lily
The Occupation
The Lifeline
Past Encounters
Pleasing Mr Pepys
A Plague on Mr Pepys
Entertaining Mr Pepys

Printed in Great Britain
by Amazon